The Case of the Birthday Bracelet

ANGELA ELWELL HUNT

THOMAS NELSON PUBLISHERS
Nashville

Published in Nashville, Tennessee, by Thomas Nelson, Inc., Publishers, and distributed in Canada by Word Communications, Ltd., Richmond, British Columbia, and in the United Kingdom by Word (UK), Ltd., Milton Keynes, England.

Library of Congress Cataloging-in-Publication Data

Hunt, Angela Elwell, 1957–
The case of the birthday bracelet / Angela Elwell Hunt.
p. cm. — (Nicki Holland mysteries : 7)
Summary: While Nicki and her friends are in England celebrating Laura's birthday, Laura's diamond bracelet disappears and it is up to the girls to try to find it.
ISBN 0-8407-6303-4 (pb)
[1. Mystery and detective stories. 2. England—Fiction.]
I. Title. II. Series: Hunt, Angela Elwell, 1957– Nicki Holland mysteries : 7.
PZ7.H9114Can 1993
[Fic]—dc20 93-11183
CIP
AC

Printed in the United States of America

1 2 3 4 5 6 7 98 97 96 95 94 93

Dedication:

For Nathan and Benji

Laura
Kim
Nicki

BEN-AMI
Meredith
Christine

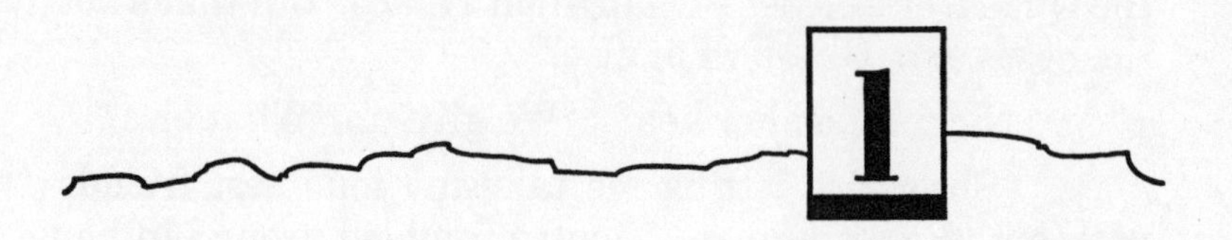

I'm glad you're all here because I've got big news," Laura Cushman announced as she made her entrance into the Hollands' comfortable den. "Guess what I'm getting for my birthday?"

Nicki Holland looked up from the Scrabble game she had been playing with Christine Kelshaw, Meredith Dixon, and Kim Park. "I know you're dying to tell us," Nicki answered, grinning at Laura. "So go ahead before you pop."

"It's probably a Rolls Royce," Christine remarked dryly, fingering the Scrabble tiles in front of her. "Or something else expensive and useless."

"You'll be sorry you said that when you hear what it is," Laura answered, her lower lip beginning to stick out in the pout Nicki knew well. "You'll be real sorry, Christine."

"So tell us already," Meredith said, looking up impatiently. "We can't wait forever."

Laura whirled gracefully on her tiptoes and opened her arms wide in a flourish. "For my thirteenth birthday, my mother is giving me a trip to London!" A blush of pleasure rose to her cheeks, and her eyes shone with excitement. "Isn't that great!"

"Wow!" Kim said, blinking in astonishment. "To London? I have always wanted to go there."

"Me, too," Laura said. "I've always wanted to see the Queen, or at least Buckingham Palace. But that's not the best part. Guess what else?"

Nicki shook her head. "We give up. What else?"

"She's also letting me take my four best friends with me. Right here . . . " Laura fumbled around in her purse and whipped out a hefty envelope, " . . . are five plane tickets to London. Mom has booked all of us on an eight-day trip, and we're staying in a hotel right across the street from Buckingham Palace."

Nicki drew in her breath, and for once Christine was shocked speechless. "You're kidding," Meredith managed to mumble. "This is all some kind of joke, right?"

"No joke," Laura answered, sinking into the Hollands' worn but comfortable overstuffed chair. Her dimples deepened as she thrust the envelope toward Meredith. "It's all right here—and you can see for yourself. Mama said the trip could be our last big fling before school starts."

Christine threw back her head and screamed with pure joy while Meredith and Nicki scrambled for the envelope. Nicki grabbed one of the tickets and studied it carefully. "She's not kidding," Nicki said, looking up at Kim and Christine. "These are honest-to-goodness airplane tickets, and they have our names on them."

"If your parents say it's okay, we're all set," Laura said, gleefully twirling a long strand of her blonde hair around her finger. "There's more stuff for you all, too. As part of the tour we get travel bags and luggage tags and brochures on all the places we'll see."

"My parents will let me go," Christine said, hugging her knees. "They'd be thrilled to have one of their six kids out of the house for a while."

"My mom will think this is a wonderfully educational experience," Meredith said, still studying the airplane ticket. "I can go, I'm sure."

"My parents might hesitate to let me go alone," Kim ventured shyly. "They still think in Korean ways and do not like me to be so independent. London is very far away!"

"My mom is going with us, and we'll be in a nice hotel," Laura said, nodding to Kim. "It will be very safe, I promise."

"I'm sure my folks will let me go," Nicki said, handing the airplane ticket back to Meredith. "They could never afford to send me on their own, so I know they'll say yes. This is too great an opportunity to pass up!"

"Good," Laura said, crossing her legs primly. "You'll need to save your money, though, because even though my mom's paying for almost everything, you'll probably need some spending money."

"I've still got my money from working this summer," Christine said, referring to the weeks when the girls had worked at the neighborhood bowling alley solving *The Case of the Haunting of Lowell Lanes*. "I can use it to buy munchies! If I'm on another continent, there won't be anybody to tell me I'm eating too much junk food!"

Nicki snapped her fingers. In all the excitement she had forgotten about the bank account she had established with her summer income. "That's right, I've got almost a hundred dollars!" she said, looking eagerly at the other girls. "I'll bet you all do. We won't have to ask our parents for anything but their permission!"

"Then it's all set," Laura said, gathering the plane tickets from Meredith. "We leave for London in three weeks. Mark your calendars, and load your cameras with fresh film. We're going to have a ball!"

Nicki hefted the suitcase she had packed and repacked six times onto the scales at the airline ticket counter. Her shiny new passport was in her hand, complete with a goofy picture that she hated. "Nobody really looks like their passport or driver's license picture," the photographer had told her when he handed her the finished photo. "If you really looked that bad, you'd be too sick to travel."

"Thank goodness we don't have to show our passports very often," Nicki whispered to Kim, who stood in line behind her at the airline check-in counter. "I don't want anyone to see this ugly thing."

Kim giggled and heaved her suitcase onto the scales while Nicki gathered her ticket and passport and moved out of the way. She couldn't believe it. In half an hour, she'd be on her way to Atlanta, and then to London, England! She pinched her upper arm to make sure she wasn't dreaming.

When they all had checked their luggage, Mrs. Cushman herded the girls to gate B32 and then walked to a nearby gift shop to buy a magazine. As she walked away, Laura leaned forward and whispered, "Mama promised she won't bug us. We could actually pretend we're on a trip completely by ourselves. Isn't this great?"

"Uh huh," Christine agreed, opening her small travel bag. She pulled out a crinkly cellophane wrapper. "Fried pork rinds, anyone?"

Meredith crinkled her nose in distaste. "Christine, I can't believe you're eating that stuff. We'll be eating *well* on the plane and in England, so why are you bringing that trash food?"

"English crumpets and tea," Laura added. "And fresh-baked scones. I'll be lucky if I don't gain ten pounds."

"You don't have to worry about your weight," Nicki

answered, giving Laura a gentle nudge with her elbow. "I know you think you're fat, but you're absolutely fine."

"Not as fine as Princess Diana," Laura said, pushing Christine's bag of fried pork rinds away. "She's beautiful, and she's thin. I want to look just like her some day. In fact," Laura lowered her voice and leaned closer to Nicki, "I have this dream, you know, that we do something great in England and we get to have an audience with the Queen. I'd do anything to meet her or Princess Diana."

Nicki, Meredith, and Christine whooped in delight, and Kim covered her mouth modestly and giggled. "I don't think it's so funny," Laura answered. "Anything could happen, you know."

"Anything could happen," Nicki agreed, looking around at the other people in the waiting area. "We could even find another mystery to solve."

"I hope not," Meredith said, shaking her head. "This is my vacation. I want to spend every free hour in the British Museum. They have a fabulous collection of Egyptian mummies. I've brought my notebook, and I'm taking notes on everything—"

"Ugh," Laura shuddered. "You can look at dead bodies if you want to, Meredith, but I'm going to London for two things—to see the crown jewels and to shop at Harrods. I can die happy if I've done those two things."

Mrs. Virginia Louise Cushman walked up and eyed the girls suspiciously. "I don't know what you've been up to," she said, her tones gently Southern. "But y'all aren't going to give me any trouble on this trip, are you?"

"No ma'am," Laura answered. "This may be the calmest, quietest week of your life, Mama."

Mrs. Cushman laughed. "Somehow I doubt that," she said.

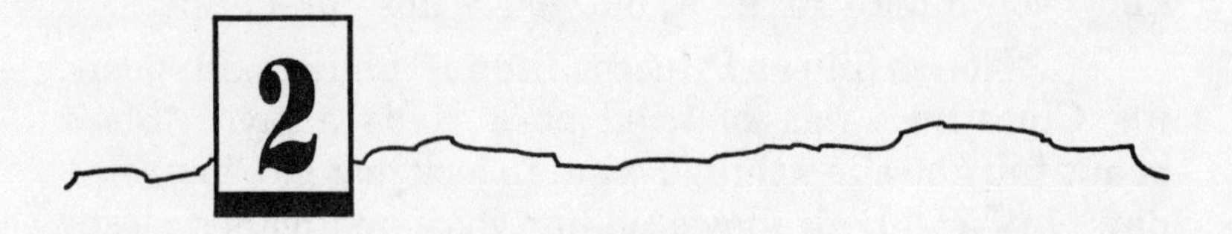

The girls were seated in a long center row in the middle of the plane, while Mrs. Cushman sat in the forward first-class section. "This is great," Christine said, looking around. "We're by ourselves and right in front of the movie screen! There's a movie, you know, on flights over the ocean."

"Transatlantic flights," Meredith interrupted offhandedly as she jotted down notes in her black notebook. "Learn the proper term, Chris—it's a *transatlantic* flight."

"Thank you, Miss Encyclopedia," Christine answered sarcastically. "My life just wasn't complete without that bit of information."

"Be quiet, you guys, the airplane guy is coming this way," Laura whispered, slinking down in her seat. "And boy, is he good-looking! I'll die if he talks to me!"

The handsome purser did pause by the girls' row and offered a stack of stiff cards to Laura. "Would you like a menu?" he said, his friendly smile bringing a blush to Laura's cheek. "I'm in a bit of a rush, so would you mind passing these down the row?"

Laura nodded wordlessly and took the menus, passing them to the other girls. When the purser had moved on, she exhaled loudly and turned to Nicki. "I'll die if I have to sit here, Nicki. Every time he hands me something, I'll croak. Trade places with me, will you?"

"No way," Nicki said, adjusting the strap on her seat belt. "I'm settled. You'll just have to learn, Laura, that you're not going to die every time a fine-looking guy talks to you."

"Look at this menu," Christine squealed, drawing the girls' attention to the cards in their hands. "Salads with romaine lettuce, croutons, and Parmesan cheese complemented by pepper cream dressing. Does that sound awful or what?"

"It sounds delicious," Laura said, frowning at Christine. "Your tastes have got to grow up, Christine. Not everyone eats pizza and hamburgers at every meal."

"Filet mignon with caper butter presented with baked potato and cheese," Meredith read from the menu. "Or breast of chicken with paprika sauce accompanied by yellow and white rice, and green beans with mushrooms and carrots."

"Black Forest cake for dessert," Kim added. "And cheese and crackers. It all sounds wonderful!"

"I'd still rather have pizza," Christine grumbled. "I just hope they have it in England, or I'll go through pepperoni withdrawal."

"Speaking of pepperoni," Laura said, her head sticking out into the aisle as she peered into the first-class section. "You'll never guess who's sitting by my mother. You know that gorgeous Italian actor on that new TV show, *Talbot Circle*? You know, Angelo Musetti? I promise, he's sitting up there by my mom."

"You're kidding." Nicki leaned over to the side, but from her seat she couldn't see anything.

"After we take off, we can all walk up there to see Mama, and I promise you'll see him, too," Laura said, waving her manicured fingernails in the air. "Maybe we can get autographs."

"Maybe he signed up for the same tour we did," Nicki offered. "You know, everyone who signed up for our tour is on this plane and will be staying at our hotel, but I guess we won't know who those people are until we get there. But if Angelo Musetti is on our tour, he'll be in our hotel—"

"He'll be visiting the same places we will—" Laura added.

"He'll be on our plane home," Kim said.

"—and maybe he'll eat breakfast, lunch, and dinner with us!" Christine squealed. "We might actually be touring London with the hottest new star on TV!"

"It's something to think about," Nicki said, turning her attention to the flight attendant who stood demonstrating the plane's safety equipment. While the flight attendant pointed to floating cushion seats and compartments for oxygen masks, Nicki dreamed about sightseeing with Angelo Musetti. While she dreamed, the plane taxied out onto the runway, the engines roared, and Nicki and her friends flew out of the United States on their way to London.

After dinners of filet mignon (only Christine had the chicken, grumbling again about how she really wanted pizza), Nicki and her friends unbuckled their seat belts and looked around the cabin. The plane was full of all kinds of people—businessmen in suits who were working out of open briefcases, women with small children already asleep on their laps, and older people who looked as if they were on vacation.

"Of all these people," Nicki whispered to Meredith and Kim, "who do you think will be on the tour with us?"

Meredith gently inclined her head toward a young

couple who obviously had eyes only for each other. "I vote for Mr. and Mrs. Newlywed," she said, whispering back. "Wouldn't a trip to England be the perfect honeymoon?"

"I don't know if they will be on our tour, but have you noticed the older man and the girl several rows behind us?" Kim asked quietly. "They have been speaking in sign language. The man is deaf, I think, and the girl has been speaking for him to the flight attendant."

Nicki looked around. Sure enough, in a back row near the window, an elderly gentleman sat with a teen-aged girl. Their faces were animated and their voices silent, but their hands flew through the air expressively as they spoke to each other in sign language.

"I have always wanted to learn how to do that," Kim whispered. "A moving language—it is really very beautiful."

Nicki wanted to watch them more, but the plane took a sudden jolt just as a gentle bell rang. "Ladies and gentleman, the pilot has requested that you return to your seats and fasten your seat belts," a flight attendant announced. "We are experiencing slight turbulence."

Nicki and her friends went back to their seats and belted themselves in. "We might as well get some sleep," Meredith told her. "I know it's nine o'clock at night to us, but in England it's two o'clock in the morning. If we don't want to be absolutely zonked tomorrow, we should all take a nap."

There was little else to do, so Nicki reached for the small white pillow and dark blanket the airline provided. Even though she was on the adventure of her life, eventually sleep came nudging in among her thoughts. As the engines roared high above the black waters of the evening Atlantic, Nicki dreamed that she and Angelo Musetti were speaking sign language together.

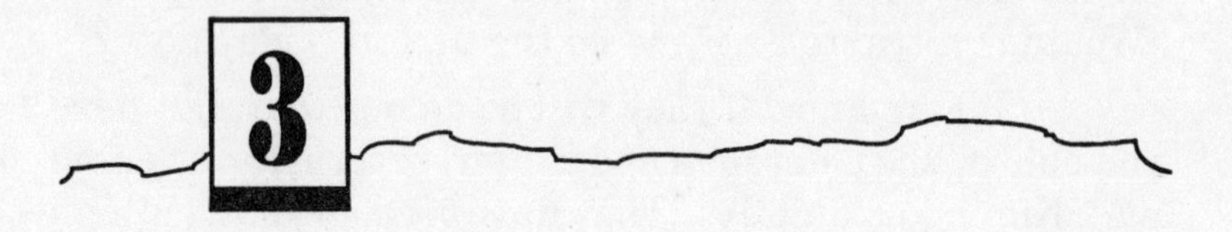

3

A slight commotion in the airplane's cabin woke Nicki, and she looked up to see a flight attendant pushing a food cart up the aisle ahead of her. "What is it?" she mumbled, half awake.

"Breakfast," Laura answered, lowering the tray table in front of her seat. "A continental breakfast: croissants, butter, fruit, jelly, and juice."

"What?" Nicki lifted her head and rubbed her eyes. "Didn't we eat just a couple of hours ago?"

"Yes," Meredith answered. "But tell your body that last meal was on American time. Now we're on London time, and it's time for breakfast."

Nicki lowered her head to peer across the aisle and through the airplane window. It was totally dark outside, but a thin navy blue line seemed to separate the darkness of the earth below from the inky sky above.

"That's the horizon," Meredith said from behind Nicki's shoulder. "Pretty soon you'll see the sun, because we're flying right toward it. It should be a pretty sight."

"That breakfast is a pretty sight," Christine said, lowering her tray table. "I'm starving. They have hot tea, too—just the way to get the day started."

The girls ate their breakfast, and by the time she had finished, Nicki felt more awake. After the breakfast trays had been taken away, the flight attendants came through the aisles carrying baskets of steaming hot face towels, which they handed out with little tongs.

"What's this for?" Christine asked, looking suspiciously at her rolled-up towel.

"For wiping your face and hands," Laura answered, delicately unrolling her hot towel and applying it to her face.

Christine giggled and juggled the hot towel as Kim watched in amusement, but Nicki thought the steamy warmth of the towel felt wonderful. She lay it over her face for a moment, then wiped her cheeks and forehead. She did feel fresher.

After the towels had been collected, Nicki got up out of her seat and made her way to the bathroom, or "lavatory" as the airplane restroom was labeled. There was a line outside, and Nicki found herself standing behind the teenaged girl who had been using sign language with the older man.

The girl leaned against the lavatory wall reading a magazine, her alert green eyes flitting quickly over the page. She had gorgeous auburn hair that just touched her shoulders, and her summer sweater and jeans were a perfect fit. Nicki smiled to herself—this girl had the perfect figure Laura would die for.

"Hello," Nicki said, trying to be friendly. "My friends and I saw you using sign language with that man. Are you two traveling together?"

The girl's eyes left the pages of her magazine and flitted over Nicki carelessly, then she smiled. "He's my grandfather," she said in a voice that was Southern and as warm as the sun. "We're going to London."

"How great!" Nicki said, smiling. "My friends and I are on a tour to London too. Maybe we'll be at the same hotel. One of my friends was fascinated by your sign language. She's dying to learn some."

"Really." The girl smiled politely, turning as the door to the lavatory opened.

"I hope we'll see you later," Nicki offered. The girl paused before closing the door.

"Maybe," she answered, the clean lines of her pretty face shining in the light from the lavatory. "Excuse me now."

The girl closed the door and Nicki stood outside feeling stupid. *She probably thinks you're some kind of nosy kid*, Nicki told herself sternly. *She's so much older, probably sixteen or seventeen at least, so why should she be nice to you*? Another lavatory door opened, and Nicki waited until the woman came out, then stepped inside and bolted the door behind her. *Forget about it*, she told herself, peering at her reflection in the small mirror. *You have your real friends with you on this trip. You don't have to worry about impressing anyone else*.

The sun had risen by the time Nicki returned to her seat, and Laura, Meredith, Kim, and Christine were leaning over two little ladies in seats by the windows, trying to catch their first glimpse of the English country-side.

"It's just like I thought it'd be," Laura gushed. "Rolling green fields, huge castles, and little white rocks everywhere."

"Those aren't rocks, they're sheep and cattle," Meredith said, elbowing Laura. "Open your eyes."

"We'd better get to our seats because we'll be landing soon," Nicki said. As if on cue, the seat belt sign above her head flashed red. "Just think," Nicki went on, edging into her seat, "in less than one hour, we'll be in England."

"Birthplace of the Beatles," Kim said.

"Home of the Queen," Laura added.

"Home of scones and crumpets," Christine added, giggling.

After the plane landed, the girls joined Mrs. Cushman at the baggage claim area, then carried their luggage through the airport exit area and found themselves on a busy curb where taxis, buses, and shuttles ferried passengers off to hotels and homes.

While Mrs. Cushman hailed a cab, Nicki was surprised to feel someone grab her elbow. "Well, we made it, didn't we?" a familiar voice asked, and Nicki turned to see the auburn-haired girl from the plane standing beside her.

"Yes, we made it," Nicki answered politely.

"Such a long trip," the girl said, placing her suitcase down on the sidewalk next to Nicki's. "I didn't think we'd ever get here. Now I don't think we'll ever get to the hotel. Say, where are you staying?"

"It's the Hotel Robyns, I think," Nicki said, shrugging. "Wherever that is."

"That's great!" the girl said, smiling. "That's where my grandfather and I are staying too. We must have signed up for the same tour package after all."

"I guess so," Nicki answered, wondering why the girl had suddenly turned into a chatterbox.

The girl cocked her head, then smiled gently, an "aw, shucks" look on her face. "Listen, I'm sorry if I seemed a little rude this morning when you spoke to me," she said. "I guess I wasn't quite awake yet, or maybe it was jet lag."

"That's okay," Nicki said, feeling a little better. "I guess we are all a little tired. I'm just too excited to feel tired right now."

"Me, too," the girl said agreeably. "So, why are you all in London? Are you a group of models or something?"

Nicki felt herself blushing, and she knew that the girl's question had been overheard by the others because Christine burst out in a loud laugh.

"No, we're not models, we're just friends. Laura's mom—the lady who's with us—planned this trip in honor of Laura's birthday. It's sort of a before school fling."

"Laura's mother must just be very generous," the girl said. "And very rich."

"She's okay," Nicki said, nodding in agreement.

A big black cab pulled over to the curb, and the girls stared in disbelief. The steering wheel was on the right-hand side of the car.

"It's backwards!" Christine squealed. "They not only drive on the wrong side of the road, but the steering wheel is backwards!"

"They don't drive on the wrong side, they drive on the *left* side," Meredith said, gently rebuking Christine. "Maybe they think we drive on the wrong side of the road."

The cab driver smiled at the girls. "The 'otel Robyns, 'ey?" he asked, a merry gleam in his eye. "I'll just flip open the boot of the car, and 'ave you there in a jiff."

"I thought they spoke English here," Kim said slowly. "What's a boot? What's an *otel*?"

"England and America are two countries separated by a common language," Meredith said, lugging her suitcase toward the cab. "At least that's what my dad says. Come on, Kim, you'll get used to it. With your quick ear, by tomorrow you'll probably be speaking English better than we speak American."

Nicki turned to the girl standing by her side. "I'm

Nicki Holland," she said, extending her hand awkwardly. "I hope we get to spend some time with you this week."

"Me, too," the girl answered, dropping her gigantic purse to shake Nicki's hand. "I'm Krisha Peterson. And while it's fun to travel with my grandfather, I know I'd like to spend some time with people more my own age, you know?"

Nicki felt herself blushing. How old did this girl think they were? She'd probably leave them in the dust if she knew they were only in middle school. "Okay," Nicki answered. "Well, we'll see you around the hotel."

"Sure." The girl picked up her suitcase as if to move away, then a look of distress crossed her face. "I can't believe it, but I've lost my grandfather in the crowd. Do you see him anywhere?"

Nicki stood on tiptoe, but there was no sign of the man. "I'm sorry, but I didn't get a good look at him on the plane," Nicki confessed. "But he wouldn't leave you, would he?"

"Yes, he would," Krisha said. "You see, he's very proud. I don't like him to go off without me because he needs me to translate for him. But he doesn't like to feel that I'm his babysitter, so he goes off alone as much as he can."

"He would just *leave* you?" Christine asked, turning to Krisha. "All alone?"

"I've traveled in Europe a lot," Krisha said, lifting her chin proudly. "I'm not afraid to go anywhere by myself."

"So how will your grandfather tell the cab driver where he wants to go?" Laura asked, jumping into the conversation. "And I'm Laura. It's nice to meet you."

"The birthday girl," Krisha answered, smiling broadly. "And you don't have to worry about Grandpa because he just writes things out on his note pad. And he doesn't worry about me. He just loves to give me the slip."

"Well, if you're going to our hotel, you might as well ride in our cab," Laura offered. "Throw your suitcase in the trunk—excuse me, the *boot*, and we'll give you a lift."

"That'd be great." Krisha handed her suitcase to the cab driver and squeezed into the back seat with Christine, Laura, Kim, and Mrs. Cushman. Nicki and Meredith joined the driver in the front.

"A lucky bloke I am, with a car full of beauties," the driver said, grinning as he got into the car. He flicked a switch on the meter and pulled away from the curb. Nicki felt strange sitting in the front left-hand seat—where her mom and dad always sat to drive. But as they pulled away from the airport and drove on the motorway through the English countryside, she forgot about the weird feeling and craned her neck to look out the window.

"This place is just gorgeous," Laura said, leaning forward. "Look at all the flowers! Every house has a rose garden in the front yard and window boxes on every window."

"I love all the stone and brick houses," Christine said. "None of that stucco or concrete block like we have at home. I'd love to live in one of these places."

"You forget, most of our houses are new," Mrs. Cushman answered. "Some of these houses are over a hundred years old, and Florida's building boom began only about thirty years ago. We don't have anything to compare with this, but we haven't been around as long, either."

"Yeah, it takes time to grow character," Laura added. "Just ask my mom."

Mrs. Cushman raised a delicate eyebrow. "Are you saying I'm old, honey?"

"No, Mama," Laura answered, laughing. "Just that you've got *loads* of character."

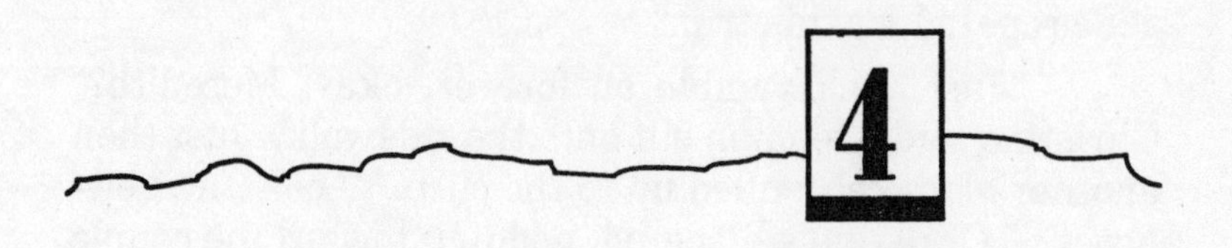

The cab driver let them out at the Hotel Robyns on Buckingham Palace Road. The hotel was located right in front of a large, walled complex the cab driver called the Royal Mews.

"What's a Royal Mews?" Laura asked, crinkling her nose. "It sounds like a home for the Queen's cats."

"You're close," Meredith answered. "The Royal Mews is the place where the Queen's horses and carriages are kept. We'll be right across the street from the Queen's thirty horses, her five Rolls Royce limousines, and her collection of state coaches." Meredith lifted her hand and began counting on her fingers. "There's the gold state coach, built in 1762 and used at every coronation since that of King George the Fourth, the glass bridal coach used by Princess Diana at her wedding, and the Australian State Coach used to take the Queen to the State Opening of Parliament. The coaches—"

"That's enough," Laura interrupted. "You've been reading again."

"Of course," Meredith sniffed, tossing her head back. "You didn't think I'd come to England without learning about all this stuff, do you? What's the fun of looking at old buildings if you don't know what you're looking at?"

"Meredith has a point," Nicki said, shouldering her

purse and gripping her carry-on bag. "I think we'll be glad she prepared for this trip."

"Just don't ramble on forever, okay, Meredith?" Christine said, stepping out onto the sidewalk. Just then another black cab pulled up to the curb. "Look, the newlyweds," Christine whispered, nodding toward the couple in the back seat of the cab. "I guess they're on our tour, too."

"Probably, but we're not going to bother them," Mrs. Cushman said, motioning for a bellman to pick up her luggage. She turned to pay the cab driver, then smiled at the girls. "Are we ready to make ourselves at home?" she asked, then led the way into the hotel lobby.

"I'm sorry, but your rooms will not be ready for another half hour," the clerk behind the desk told Mrs. Cushman. "We will have your rooms ready at half past."

Nicki was ready to giggle at the young woman's pronunciation of "half past" as "hoff pahst," but she bit her lip when she saw that Mrs. Cushman's smile had wilted. "Maybe we could sit in the restaurant and have a cup of tea," Nicki suggested, trying to help.

Mrs. Cushman smiled wearily. "Send the bags up to our rooms, please, when the rooms are ready," she instructed the clerk. "We'll be in the restaurant having brunch."

Nicki glanced around the hotel lobby. The honeymoon couple snuggled on the love seat, oblivious to everyone else, and Krisha stood nearby, her face frozen in a perplexed look. Suddenly the lobby doors opened and a neatly dressed bald man entered. He carried a single leather suitcase in one hand and a handsome carved walking stick in the other.

"Grandpa!" Krisha exclaimed. She dropped her luggage and hurried toward the man as his face brightened in a wide grin.

"He looks like he really pulled a fast one on her," Laura whispered in Nicki's ear. "Can you believe he would leave her at the airport like that?"

Nicki shook her head. "It takes all kinds of people to make the world go round," she said, watching Krisha converse with her grandfather in a flurry of sign language.

As they flashed signs back and forth for several minutes, Nicki watched, fascinated. The man smiled and nodded, and Krisha smiled and nodded while they "talked," then Krisha turned to Nicki. "My grandfather noticed us together and was congratulating me on my choice of friends." She sighed and shrugged her shoulders. "Well, I guess I'll say goodbye to you all now. It sure was nice to meet you, almost as fun as bunking together would be."

"That would be fun!" Nicki said, turning to Laura. "Wouldn't it Laura?"

Nicki jerked her head towards Krisha, and Laura took the hint. "Sure, Krisha, since you're staying here in our hotel, why don't you stay in our room? It'd be like a slumber party."

"That would be delightful," Mrs. Cushman inserted. "I wouldn't worry about you girls if you had someone older with you."

Krisha beamed in pleasure. "Let me check with Grandpa," she said, turning to the very old gentleman. Her hands flew in a flurry of signs, the man nodded and responded, and Krisha turned back to the girls. "He says it's okay, and he thanks you."

"He's welcome," Mrs. Cushman replied. "Now come

with us for a cup of tea. Your grandfather can come too, if he likes."

"He wants to wait for his room," Krisha answered. She waved goodbye to her grandfather and followed Mrs. Cushman.

Nicki turned and followed the others, but once she glanced back at Krisha's grandfather as he waited in the lobby. It seemed to her that he was laughing at them.

What in the world was so funny?

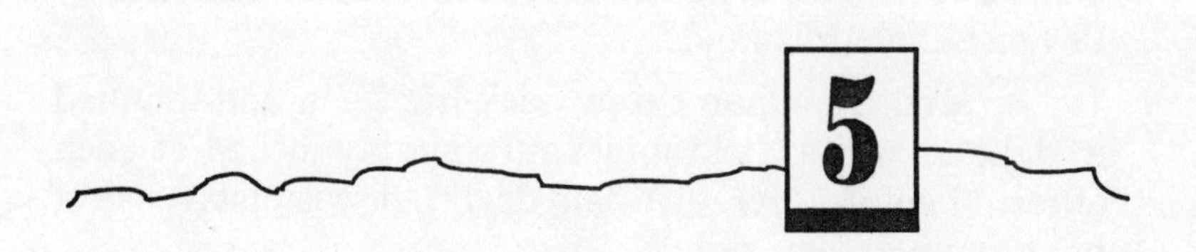

5

Nicki whistled in appreciation as they were seated at a large round table in the hotel restaurant. A lovely arrangement of summer flowers graced the center of the table, and as Nicki unfolded the crisp linen napkin at her place, she caught Meredith's eye and winked. "We're a long way from McDonald's in Pine Grove, aren't we?" she whispered. Meredith nodded solemnly in response.

Mrs. Cushman ordered Shepherd's Pie for all of them, and Nicki had to steel herself to keep from making a face. She didn't know what Shepherd's Pie was and she didn't think she'd like it, but it would have been rude to object to Mrs. Cushman's choice. After all, without Mrs. Cushman's generosity, none of them would even be there.

Nicki elbowed Krisha, who sat next to her. "What's Shepherd's Pie and is it good?" Nicki whispered. "I've never had it."

"It's a little like a stew with mashed potatoes on top," Krisha whispered back, grinning. "You'll like it. That reminds me," she went on, speaking to the group. "I heard a story once about a man who was famous for making a great dish called Poy. A gourmet heard about the man and his Poy, and he searched all over the world until he finally found the Poy man in a remote Himalayan village. 'It's amazing that you've never had Poy,' the man told the gourmet, 'because a man from London gave me the recipe. But since you have come all this way, I'll gladly make Poy for you. What would you like, Steak and Kidney Poy or Shepherd's Poy?'"

Mrs. Cushman threw back her head and laughed in delight, while Nicki and Laura simply looked at each other. "I get it," Meredith said dryly, "it was just a case of mispronunciation, right?"

"It was his accent," Krisha said, laughing along with Mrs. Cushman. "Shepherd's Pie—Shepherd's Poy!"

Nicki smiled politely and decided to enjoy her first meal in England whether it was pie or poy. After all, she was on the dream trip of her life with her four best pals and an exciting new friend. What could go wrong?

After the Shepherd's Pie, cups of hot tea, and pastries for dessert, Mrs. Cushman gently cleared her throat and pushed back the bangs of her soft apricot-colored hair. "As y'all know, this trip is in honor of Laura's birthday," she said smoothly, her Southern accent sounding slow and luxurious in the midst of the clipped English tones around them. "And since I gave birth to this little gem thirteen years ago today, she's been a bright and shining jewel in my life. Here's a little token of my love for you, Laura dear."

From her purse, Mrs. Cushman pulled out a velvet jewel case, which she handed to Laura. Laura bent forward and kissed her mother on the cheek, then opened the box. A row of diamonds twinkled against the dark blue velvet of the box.

"A diamond tennis bracelet," Laura squealed, her face turning pink with pleasure. "Oh Mama, it's beautiful!"

"It's your first really good piece of jewelry—you're growing up now," Mrs. Cushman said, gently fingering the bracelet with her manicured fingernail. "Take good care of it, honey. I hope you enjoy wearing it."

Laura lifted the bracelet out of the case and slipped it over her arm. Christine eagerly reached out to fasten the clasp, then Laura held her arm up so everyone could see it. Nicki didn't know much about jewelry, but she could tell from the brightness of the glittering stones that Mrs. Cushman's gift to Laura was valuable.

"I hope you have that insured," Krisha remarked to Mrs. Cushman, her eyes never leaving the diamond bracelet. "I'd hate for her to lose it in London."

"Don't worry," Mrs. Cushman answered, dismissing Krisha's concern with a wave of her dainty hand. "Everything's been taken care of."

Laura giggled and rubbed the bracelet against her cheek. "I love it, Mama," she said simply, holding it up again so that the diamonds glittered in the light. "I absolutely *adore* it."

Just then a handsome young man Nicki had noticed in the lobby stepped forward and handed Mrs. Cushman a red rose. "Excuse me, I do not mean to interrupt your lunch," he said, his delightful English accent turning every head in his direction. "I am Gregory, the hotel concierge. I am sorry that your rooms were not ready when you arrived, but I'm pleased to tell you they are ready and waiting now."

"That's wonderful," Mrs. Cushman answered, rising gracefully from her chair. "We would appreciate it if you would have our bags sent up."

"They are in your rooms already," Gregory said, bowing his head respectfully to Mrs. Cushman. His dark eyes danced as he looked around their table. "It is a pleasure to serve such lovely ladies."

When he turned and left, Laura sighed dramatically. "He's *gorgeous*," she whispered, forgetting all about her bracelet. "How old do you think he is?"

"What's a concierge?" Christine asked, her eyes wide. "Will we see him again?"

"A concierge is a hotel staff member who handles luggage and mail, makes reservations, arranges tours, and usually speaks several languages," Meredith replied automatically. "It's from the French word for *fellow slave*."

"He's our slave?" Christine grinned wickedly. "Oh, boy!"

"Not exactly," Nicki answered. "Calm down, Chris."

Nicki excused herself from the table and made her way to the hotel rest room. As she washed her hands, a young woman came in and proceeded to brush her brown hair and reapply her lipstick. Nicki blushed when the woman caught her eye in the mirror.

"I didn't mean to stare," Nicki said, feeling her cheeks burning. "It's just that you look familiar, and I don't know anyone in England."

"We were on the plane together," the woman said with a graceful toss of her head. "My husband and I sat across the aisle from you and your friends."

"You're one of the newlyweds," Nicki cried, remembering. "I didn't recognize you without your husband."

The woman smiled. "I just hope you and your friends have a better beginning to your trip than we did."

"What happened?" Nicki asked, drying her hands on a linen towel

"While we were on the plane, someone stole a handful of traveler's checks right out of my purse," the bride explained. "I suppose it was foolish to put my purse in the overhead compartment, but I just wasn't thinking. I've heard that tourists are easy prey for pickpockets, purse snatchers, you name it."

"Brother," Nicki exclaimed, leaning against the sink. "I guess we had better be careful."

The young woman nodded. "I think you had better."

"Thanks," Nicki called, leaving the rest room. "I'll warn my friends."

She had just told her story to the girls waiting by the elevator when Kim pointed toward the lobby "There's your grandfather, Krisha. Why don't you officially introduce us? Can you teach me the sign for 'hello'?"

A look of irritation crossed Krisha's face, but then she nodded and walked toward her grandfather. She caught his eye and began signing furiously, then she motioned for the girls to come over. "I don't want to embarrass him by giving you a long sign language lesson now," she told the girls, "but 'hello' is simple—you just move your hand from your forehead like you're saluting."

"My first word in sign language," Kim whispered, practicing her salute in a mirror by the elevator. "Hello."

The girls all saluted the man awkwardly, but that wasn't enough for Mrs. Cushman. "Krisha, dear, I'm simply not going to stand here and merely salute the man," she said, stepping forward. "What's your grandfather's name? Does he read lips at all?"

"His name is, uh, Duane Smithson," Krisha stammered, obviously surprised by Mrs. Cushman's insistence.

"Mr. Smithson, it's a pleasure to meet you," Mrs.

Cushman said, reaching for his hand and pumping it firmly. Still holding his hand, she turned to Krisha. "What does he do? Where is he from?"

"Uh, he's a retired bus mechanic," Krisha answered, her face turning bright red. "From Mansfield, Ohio."

"That's nothing to be ashamed of," Mrs. Cushman told Krisha. She pumped Mr. Smithson's hand again. "Such a lovely granddaughter you have there. I'm sure our girls will adore having her in their room."

Mr. Smithson looked at Mrs. Cushman as if she were from Pluto, then turned to Krisha, who communicated in a flurry of hand signs and gestures. Mr. Smithson nodded, then gently released his hand from Mrs. Cushman's friendly grasp and pointed to Laura. Then he signed something, and pointed again to Laura, but this time he pointed specifically to her birthday bracelet.

"He says your bracelet is lovely," Krisha interpreted.

"Thank him for me," Laura said, her eyes as bright as the diamonds in her bracelet.

"You can thank him yourself," Krisha answered. "Just put your fingers to your chin, palms facing your face, then pull both your hands out from your face about six inches."

Krisha demonstrated, and Laura copied the sign. Mr. Smithson beamed.

"I must learn to speak this language," Kim whispered to Nicki. "Look what pleasure it brings."

Mrs. Cushman waved goodbye to Mr. Smithson and led the girls toward the elevators. "He's a lovely man," she said as the girls joined her. "Lovely soft hands. Quiet manners. Refined. I would never have guessed him to be a bus mechanic, but don't you be embarrassed, Krisha

The world needs people who make a living with their hands. We can't all be bankers and stockbrokers."

Nicki hoped Mrs. Cushman's prattle about mechanics and bankers wasn't hurting Krisha's feelings, but the older girl didn't even seem to be listening. She was steadily staring at the concierge's desk, probably hoping to catch a glimpse of Gregory.

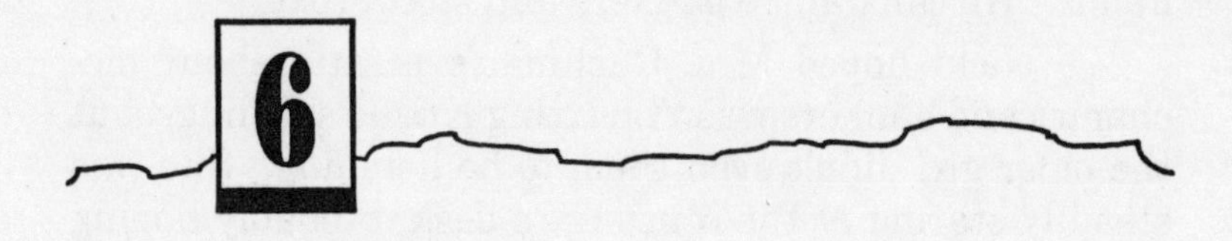

In the elevator, Mrs. Cushman gave each of them a thin plastic card. "This is your room key," she explained, "so don't lose it. And whenever you enter your room, immediately lock the dead bolt. You can never be too careful about personal security in a hotel."

Nicki found her luggage in a room with Kim's and Meredith's, but their room was connected to an adjoining room where Christine, Laura, and Krisha were staying.

"Isn't this great?" Christine said, coming through the door into Nicki's room and plopping onto the nearest twin bed. "Did you turn on the TV? The commercials are a scream! People talk about eating breakfast cereals I've never heard of, and cleaning with detergents I've never seen before."

"This is another country," Meredith said patiently, lugging her heavy suitcase to the bed where Christine reclined. "And would you mind moving? I'd like to unpack and I need this bed."

"You're an awful grouch today, Meredith," Christine answered, rolling off Meredith's bed and perching on Nicki's. "Why unpack at all? I live out of my suitcase. If you don't unpack, you won't have to pack again when it's time to go home."

"And you'll be wrinkled everywhere you go," Nicki added, laughing. "Come on, Chris, don't you think you should unpack a few things?"

"Nope," Christine answered. "All I brought was jeans and sweaters, and they don't wrinkle."

"Did you see the bathroom?" Kim came into the room, her eyes wide. "The toilet is tall and the seat is round. And there is a basket with shampoo and conditioner, a sewing kit, a shower cap, perfumed body gel, and several little soaps."

"Except for the toilet, it sounds just like home," Nicki said, laughing. "Except that my little brother and sister usually leave wet towels on the floor."

Meredith drew back the drapes and lifted the heavy window. The room looked out onto a courtyard several stories below them, and somewhere a radio played a Phil Collins song.

"It just *feels* like England," Meredith breathed. "The air is cooler, the breeze is gentle—"

"Are you sleeping with that window open?" Christine interrupted. She frowned. "There are no screens on the windows, for heaven's sake."

"There aren't any bugs," Nicki pointed out. "This isn't Florida, Chris."

"And no one can come in," Meredith pointed out. "We're four stories above ground and there is no ledge or fire escape nearby. We could have the window wide open and we'd be safe."

"Let's do it," Kim said eagerly. "It has been so hot at home, it would be wonderful to sleep in fresh air."

"I second the motion," Nicki added. "So Christine, if you don't want to keep the window open, stay in your room with Krisha and Laura. You guys can suffocate in there if you want to."

"Maybe we will," Christine sniffed.

Laura interrupted the debate by sticking her head through the doorway. "We're leaving for the bus tour," she called gaily. "Come on, let's not miss a minute."

Nicki, Meredith, Kim, and Christine forgot about unpacking and made a mad dash for cameras and purses. Nicki pocketed the credit card room key, and in a moment they were all out the door.

They boarded an open double-decker tour bus outside their hotel and settled into the upper-level seats. "I hope it doesn't rain," Kim said, looking up at the blue sky above them. "I've never been on a bus without a roof before."

"This is the real way to see London," Laura said, flashing a smile at the young man who stood at the microphone. "We'll drive by everything important, and then we can choose the things we want to go back and see."

The bus engine roared to life, the young man picked up his microphone, and for the next ninety minutes the girls learned all about the House of Parliament, Westminster Abbey, St. Paul's Cathedral, the Tower Bridge, the Globe Theatre, Buckingham Palace, and the City of London. "The Queen is not allowed to visit the City of London without permission from the City's mayor," the tour guide said. "This one-square-mile city has its own constitution and elects its own lord mayor. It is one of the world's foremost financial, commercial, industrial, and cultural centers."

"I thought the Queen lived in London," Nicki remarked, crinkling her nose. "I never dreamed she wouldn't be allowed to even *enter* it."

"Actually what we think of as London is The City with several smaller communities near it," Meredith explained. "The British kings and queens made the City of Westminster their seat of power."

Krisha leaned forward and tapped Nicki's shoulder. "I take it Meredith is smart," she remarked.

Nicki rolled her eyes. "Slightly. She's probably a genius. Both of her parents are college professors."

"I hate smart people," Krisha said abruptly, then she eased back into her seat, frowning.

Nicki faced forward to see the monument the tour guide was describing, but she was more than a little disturbed. She and her friends had never been bothered by Meredith's brains. What did Krisha have against smart people?

The sight-seeing bus dropped them off at their hotel, and Mrs. Cushman consulted her diamond-studded watch. "I think if we hurry, we can make Kensington Palace for the Court Couture display," she said. "They show ball gowns designed for this season, plus I understand that Princess Diana's wedding dress is on display there. Why don't we meet down here in fifteen minutes?"

"Great!" Laura said, and she led the girls into the elevator while Mrs. Cushman paused at the desk to take care of some business. Krisha stopped by the elevator door. "Go on up without me," she said. "I need to find out what room my grandfather's in. I feel guilty just going off and leaving him like this."

Nicki shrugged and pushed the elevator button. "See you later, then," she said.

The girls freshened up in their rooms, and Nicki pulled on a jacket. The London breezes were cooler than she had expected. Laura and Christine changed into completely different outfits, while Meredith and Kim shook their heads in bewilderment.

"I changed because Kensington Palace is where Princess Diana lives," Christine warbled as they made their way through the hall to the elevator. "What if we run into her? We could actually *see* her, you know, and maybe she'll invite us for tea or something. Wouldn't that be a hoot?"

"You're dreaming," Meredith said, snapping her fingers in front of Christine's face. "Princesses do not mix with tourists."

"You never know," Laura replied airily. "I have a special feeling about this trip."

"If she sees your diamond bracelet, she might think you are a princess," Kim offered.

"That's right," Laura said, holding up her wrist. Suddenly she stopped so suddenly that Nicki nearly ran into her. "My bracelet!" Laura gasped. "It's gone!"

"It's not, you had it on just a little while ago," Christine answered, grabbing Laura's arm.

They all stared in silence at Laura's bony wrist. "You're right, it's gone," Nicki whispered. "Where did you drop it?"

"It must have fallen off in the room," Laura said, her eyes filling with tears. "Can we go back and look for it? And whatever you do, please don't tell my mother I lost it. She'd kill me."

"If we go back and look for it now we'll be late meeting your mother," Meredith pointed out. "And she'll want to know why."

Laura bit her lip and pulled her long sleeves down over her wrists. "I guess it'll wait wherever it is, right? We'll just look for it when we get back."

The other girls nodded in sympathy, and they walked on toward the elevator, but their steps were heavy and slow. Nicki felt sorry for Laura and knew she'd feel terrible if she lost something so valuable just a couple of hours after her mom had given it to her. Mrs. Cushman was rich, and maybe she wouldn't miss the money that the bracelet cost, but it obviously had meant a lot to her. Laura just had to find that bracelet.

The elevator doors finally opened and Krisha, breathless, stepped out as the others entered the small elevator. "Hey, y'all wait for me, okay?" she called, hurrying past them. "I just want to put my purse in the room. Wait for me in the lobby, okay?"

"Okay," Nicki promised, then she stepped into the elevator and looked at her friends Meredith's forehead was wrinkled in concentration, Kim's eyes were wide with confusion, and Christine's arms were crossed in sulky defiance.

"You'd better find that bracelet, or you'll ruin things for all of us," Christine whispered to Laura as the elevator began its descent. "You'll be miserable, your mom will be furious, Nicki will set out on another mystery, and we won't have any fun at all. So you'd better find that bracelet, Laura Cushman!"

"Hush, Christine, it's not her fault," Nicki said, noticing that Laura looked as if she were about to cry. "Now everyone, shape up. We don't want Mrs. Cushman to know something's wrong, do we?"

The doors of the elevator parted on the ground floor, and the girls made their way out into the lobby to meet Mrs. Cushman. Nicki noticed with approval that all of them managed to smile.

While they made small talk with Mrs. Cushman, Krisha flew into the lobby from the stairs, her cheeks glowing with energy.

"I took the stairs down," she said. "It's a great way to keep in shape while you're traveling."

"You should take the stairs *up* for a better workout," Meredith observed, but Krisha ignored the comment and smiled broadly at Mrs. Cushman. "On to Kensington Palace, shall we?" she chirped. "I'm dying to get a look at the Court Couture."

"Exactly what is court couture?" Christine whispered to Meredith and Nicki as they stood inside the wood-paneled entrance to the public portion of Kensington Palace

"It's a collection of court dresses," Meredith explained, rapidly skimming over the brochure in her hand. "Court dress was the particular form of costume worn by ladies when they were presented to the monarch. Young ladies being presented had to wear a formal gown with a train, a headpiece, and gloves. Worst of all, they had to curtsy in all that getup."

The girls moved eagerly through the display, exclaiming over the old dresses and the new designs. "Here's a dress made of paper, artificial flowers, and old stamps," Christine squealed, pointing to an ultra-modern number on a mannequin.

"I like this one by Zandra Rhodes," Krisha said, pointing to an elegant gown embroidered with silver beads. "Over there, Meredith, is one you'll like, I'm sure."

"Where?" Meredith looked in the direction of Krisha's pointed finger, then returned a stony glance to the older girl. "Why should I like a dress of fiber optics and illuminated circuit boards over jersey?" Meredith demanded, her eyes flashing. "Just because I'm—"

"Skip it, Meredith," Nicki said, coming to stand between Meredith and Krisha. "I know the silk dress over here is more your type." She forced herself to laugh lightly. "Circuit boards don't do a thing for you."

The only girl who was not having a good time was Laura, who walked absently behind her mother and answered "Yes, ma'am" occasionally. Even the huge display case which featured a model of Princess Diana in the actual royal wedding dress did little to lift Laura's bad mood. Nicki knew Laura was worried sick. What if they did not find the diamond bracelet?

7

Slow down, Laura, or you'll knock somebody down," Nicki called after her friend, who broke away from the other girls as soon as they stepped out of the hotel elevator.

"I don't blame her, I'd run, too," Christine said, snapping her gum in rhythm to their steps. "My mom would absolutely freak out if she gave me diamonds and I lost them. Of course," she added, tilting her head, "my mom would have to be mental before she'd give me diamonds."

"Laura lost her bracelet?" Krisha asked, her eyes widening. "Why didn't you say anything?"

"Laura doesn't want her mother to know," Meredith answered. "And we're not sure when it happened. She noticed that the bracelet was gone just as we were leaving for Kensington Palace."

"She had just changed her clothes, so she thinks the bracelet fell on the floor," Nicki said. "It'll be there, I'm sure, if we look for it."

A shriek shattered the stillness of the quiet hallway and Nicki's heart skipped a beat. Running to the open door of their room, Nicki found Laura, pale and shaking, and a young housekeeper with a vacuum cleaner in her hand.

"Excuse me, you didn't just vacuum, did you?" Nicki asked slowly, her eyes searching the freshly fluffed carpet. "I thought the room had already been cleaned."

"It was cleaned, dearie," the pretty young woman answered, wrapping the vacuum cleaner cord around the handle, "but our concierge, Gregory, was up 'ere delivering flowers to this room and he reported that the room was a mess. 'E sent me up 'ere to clean up right away."

"Gregory delivered flowers to this room?" Meredith asked, sinking onto her bed. "Why?"

"In honor of somebody's birthday," the housekeeper answered, shrugging. She pointed over her shoulder. "There's the bouquet; see for yourself."

Laura burst into tears and threw herself on her bed, while the housekeeper stared at her in bewilderment. Nicki found herself instinctively liking this young woman—she had startling blue eyes, long curly blonde hair, and cheeks that were either naturally rosy or red from hard work.

"Excuse Laura, she's jet-lagged," Nicki said, moving out of the way so the housekeeper could leave. "She's just tired."

"What's your name, please, in case we need it," Krisha asked, stopping the housekeeper at the door.

"I don't know why you should need it," she answered, her eyes narrowing defensively. "But I'm Tilda."

"Maybe we'll want to leave you a nice tip, Tilda," Krisha replied smoothly. "For a job well done."

Tilda smiled and pushed the vacuum cleaner out the door. "That'd be lovely," she answered. "Call me if you need anything else."

The moment the door closed, Nicki, Christine, Meredith, and Kim dropped to their hands and knees to search the floor. Krisha watched them paw the carpet and shook her head. "If she vacuumed, you're not going to find anything," she said. "And I'm amazed that you've missed the obvious. If the bracelet was on the floor, it would have made a terrific racket when it got sucked up in the vacuum. Tilda would have checked to see what it was, and she would have found the bracelet. My guess is that she has the bracelet tucked right inside her neat little pocket. That's why I made sure we got her name."

Nicki sat up and crinkled her forehead in thought. "What do you think, Meredith?" she asked.

Meredith sat up, too. "If Laura had the bracelet when we came back from the tour bus—"

"Did you, Laura?" Christine asked.

"I don't remember," Laura wailed, lifting her tear-streaked face from her pillow. "The last time I remember seeing it was in the restaurant."

"I remember seeing it on your arm while we were on the bus," Kim volunteered. "The sun was shining on it, and it sparkled."

"Good," Meredith said. "Now we know it's not in the restaurant. If we assume that you dropped it when you were changing clothes, the only ones who have had opportunity to take it are the housekeeper, the concierge, and the vacuum cleaner."

"And any of us, of course," Nicki said, looking around at her friends. "Technically, we were all in this room."

"But a criminal must have opportunity *and* motive," Kim pointed out. "And none of us has a motive. None of us would want to steal Laura's birthday bracelet."

"Right," Nicki agreed. "That leaves Gregory, Tilda, and the vacuum."

"This sounds an awful lot like another mystery," Christine said, making a face. "I thought we were coming to London to have fun. Don't give us another mystery to solve, Nicki."

"I'm not giving us a mystery," Nicki protested. "I'm just trying to help Laura find her bracelet."

"But there is something mysterious going on here," Meredith pointed out. "After all, diamond bracelets don't just get up and crawl away. They have to be taken."

"Like the housekeeper," Krisha inserted.

"Like that Gregory guy," Christine said. "Why else would he come up here bringing flowers? I've stayed in hotels before, and nobody's ever brought me flowers. He knew about the bracelet, too, 'cause he saw it at lunch. The housekeeper didn't know there was a diamond bracelet on the floor in here."

"I think the vacuum cleaner ate it," Kim offered. "Tilda seemed nice, and not the type to steal. Gregory was kind and polite, not the kind of man who would steal, either."

"Then who did it?" Christine demanded.

"I did it!" Laura sobbed, beating her pillow with her fist. "It's all my fault. The bracelet's gone and first my mother's going to be mad, then she's going to be really hurt."

"We're probably jumping to conclusions," Nicki said, leaning over to pat Laura on the shoulder. "We're going to go through this room with a fine-tooth comb. We're going to empty your suitcase, look in the seams of the clothes you were wearing—"

"Check your shoes," Meredith suggested. "Maybe it fell off into your shoes."

"And the bathroom," Christine added. "We'll check all the plumbing, so nobody flush the toilet or run water in the sink until we're done."

"Well, whatever we do, we'd better do it fast," Krisha pointed out. "We're supposed to meet Laura's mom downstairs for dinner at seven-thirty. That only gives us forty-five minutes."

"We'll be quick," Nicki said. "Kim, you help Laura check through her clothes and everything in her suitcase. Christine, do you know how to check the drain of a sink?"

"Sure," Christine grinned, her freckles gleaming. "My little brothers are always washing things down the toilet and sink. I'll take care of the bathroom."

"Meredith, will you go over the floors again?" Nicki asked. "Don't forget to look under the beds and in the shoes that we've got scattered everywhere. And Krisha—"

"I think this is all kind of silly," Krisha said, arching an eyebrow. "I mean, aren't you guys a little too old to be playing Nancy Drew?"

"We're not playing anything," Nicki answered. She moved to the phone and lifted the receiver. "I'm going to call housekeeping and tell them we need Tilda's vacuum cleaner up here. I'm going to go through everything in the vacuum cleaner bag, and I'll need your help."

Krisha shook her head. "You're crazy. And if you're going to go through a dustbag, there's no way you're going to be presentable for dinner tonight. I'll go tell Mrs. Cushman that we're ordering from room service tonight."

"That's a good idea," Meredith said, looking up from the floor. "I feel too tired to eat, anyway. Remember, it's only seven o'clock here, but it feels like midnight to our bodies. We'll all get sick if we don't get some sleep."

"I can't sleep until I find my bracelet," Laura moaned. "And I can't face my mother, either, so room service is a great idea."

"Okay," Nicki agreed. "Room service it is. I just hope we find that bracelet soon!"

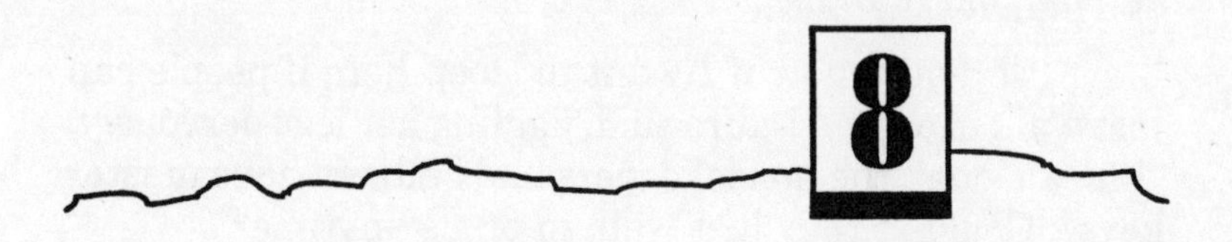

An hour later, Nicki, Meredith, Kim, Laura, and Christine sat covered in dust. The gutted vacuum cleaner bag lay open on the floor in front of them, spewing a fine layer of dust and dirt over everything. "Now Tilda will have to come in and clean again," Kim remarked. "This place is a mess!"

"Too bad Krisha is above making such a mess," Meredith noted. "Did you notice that she was the only one of us who didn't get her hands dirty?"

"We can't expect her to be one of us," Nicki said, defending her new friend. "After all, she's really here with her grandfather, not us. And she hardly knows us."

"She thinks we're immature," Laura sniffed. "She thinks we're little kids playing detective, and she knows I'm irresponsible because I lost my bracelet."

"Well, we know you didn't lose it in this room," Nicki said, gathering the edges of the vacuum cleaner bag together and dumping the contents in the trash. A cloud of dust arose, and she turned her head and sneezed.

"We've been over every inch of this room plus the vacuum cleaner, so the bracelet is simply not here," Meredith told Laura. "You either lost it on the bus, on the sidewalk between the bus and the hotel, in the elevator, the hall—"

"Or someone stole it," Christine added. "Gregory or Tilda, for instance."

"I don't know if I want to sleep here if people can just walk in on us," Laura said, jiggling her legs nervously. "I mean, don't the housekeepers and bellmen have master keys? Couldn't they just walk in on us anytime?"

"Not if we lock the dead bolt like your mother told us to," Kim pointed out. "And ours is locked now. No one can come in."

Christine snapped her fingers. "The window!" she gasped. "Maybe someone came in through the window."

Meredith shook her head. "Only someone who flies," she said. "We're four floors straight up."

Nicki scratched her head. "Are we missing any other clues?" she asked. "Was there anything strange in the room when we came back? Or was anything else missing?"

Christine shrugged. "We had begun to unpack, Nicki. Stuff was everywhere. The bathroom was a mess, and so were our beds."

"The flowers were here," Meredith said. "And I checked the card—all it said was 'Happy Birthday, Compliments of the Hotel Robyns.'"

"So Mrs. Cushman didn't order those flowers," Nicki said, thinking aloud. "It was probably Gregory's idea to bring them up."

"See there?" Christine said, standing up. "I tell you, Gregory is my number one suspect. He knew about the bracelet, he probably saw us go out, he brought the flowers in, hoping Laura had left the bracelet here, he found it, called the housekeeper in to cover his tracks, and there! The perfect crime!"

"What's Gregory going to do with a diamond bracelet?" Laura asked sarcastically. "He's much too good looking and dignified to be a thief. I don't think he would take my bracelet, Christine."

A light rap sounded on the door and they heard Krisha's warm voice. "It's me," she called. Nicki hopped up to release the dead bolt and let Krisha in.

"Are my little sleuths still working on the case?" Krisha asked, as she came into the room. "Good grief, this place is dustier than my grandpa's attic."

"We're still working, and we haven't found anything," Nicki answered. "Any suggestions?"

"Not really," Krisha answered. She walked gracefully to her bed and pulled back the dusty bedspread before stretching out. "Are you going to call the police?"

Nicki looked at Laura, but Laura gasped and put her hand to her face. "No way," she said. "Then my mother would know."

"You're going to have to tell your mom sooner or later," Meredith pointed out. "If the bracelet's covered under her insurance policy, she'll want to claim it and get her money back."

"She might even replace it," Krisha added. "Then you won't be out anything."

"Telling the police might be a good idea," Nicki said. "Then they could interview Tilda and Gregory and anyone else who might have been in the room. And we wouldn't have a mystery to solve, and we could just have fun on this trip, as Christine says."

"Okay," Laura sighed and looked down at the floor. "I'll tell Mama, but not until the day before we leave. I'll have a chance to find it before then. Or maybe you'll solve the mystery, Nicki. At least we can try!"

Nicki looked at her friend. "It's your decision,

Laura," she said. "We'll do whatever you want to do."

"I want to find my bracelet," Laura said firmly. "But right now I'm so tired I can't keep my eyes open. Let's go to bed, and maybe we'll think better in the morning."

"That sounds good," Nicki agreed, moving with Kim and Meredith toward the doorway to their adjoining room. Nicki paused before leaving Laura's room. Stretched out on her bed, Krisha was already asleep.

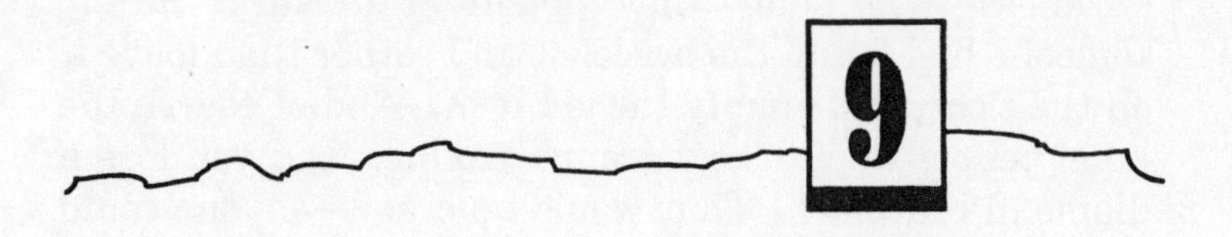

Even though she felt dead tired, Nicki could hardly sleep. The glowing hands of her travel alarm clock told her it was midnight, but she knew it was only seven o'clock back home and hardly time for bed. She could tell from the regular sounds of their breathing that Kim and Meredith were sleeping soundly, but the day's events spun round and round in Nicki's mind like a wearisome stuck record.

Was every other person in London a pickpocket or thief? Last year her school had presented songs from the movie *Oliver*, about the London orphan boy who was befriended by a gang of boys who learned to "pick a little pocket or two," but that play was set in another era. And even though her mother had warned her about leaving her purse unguarded, she didn't think her mom and dad would have let her come to London if it was really unsafe. Why, then, had she run into two cases of stealing in just one day? Maybe the new bride from the plane misplaced her traveler's checks. Maybe it was all a misunderstanding, or maybe they had been stolen back in the United States while the couple waited to board the plane.

And maybe Laura's bracelet just had a weak clasp that gave way as she walked through the hotel lobby. Maybe someone picked it up, and even now it was downstairs in a fancy lost and found, just waiting for Laura to come and claim it. That was it!

Nicki sat straight up in bed, her eyes shining in the darkness. Why hadn't they thought of it before? Surely someone had found the bracelet, and rather than leave it on the floor, had simply turned it in. And of course the hotel people wouldn't go around asking, "Did you lose a diamond bracelet?" That would be crazy—anyone could claim it. The hotel people probably had the bracelet right now in a safe, waiting for Laura to show up and ask for it.

"We'll go down first thing in the morning," Nicki whispered, punching her pillow to get comfortable. "Laura will have her bracelet back before breakfast, and everyone will be happy." Nicki put her hands behind her head and settled back into her pillow. Thinking happier thoughts, she soon fell asleep.

"Good grief, I look as bad as a passport picture," Krisha groaned, staring into the mirror.

Nicki opened her eyes slowly and was surprised to see that the sun had already risen high and was peering through her window. Krisha stood in Nicki's room, fluffing her messy hair as she studied her reflection. She caught Nicki's eye in the mirror. "Hey, Nick, do you have some shampoo I can borrow? Christine used all the complimentary shampoo, and Laura doesn't exactly seem thrilled at the thought of me using her essence-of-gardenia hair products."

Nicki shook the cloud of sleep from her head and threw her covers off. "Sure, just let me get to my suitcase," she mumbled. "Hey, and you're wrong about your passport picture. You look great in the morning. You ought to see my passport picture."

Nicki fished her passport out of her purse and tossed it to Krisha, who looked at the picture and made a suitably impressed face. Nicki had her shampoo in her hand, but she suddenly clutched it tightly and pulled it away from Krisha. "You gotta give me something before I let you have this," she said, her eyes twinkling. "Fair is fair. I let you see my mug shot, now you have to let me see yours."

Krisha's brows knitted into a frown, and her mouth drooped at the corners. "No way," she said firmly. "Absolutely no way."

"Come on," Nicki said, sensing that Krisha was becoming defensive. "It can't be as bad as all that. After all, you're so pretty, I'll bet you can't take a bad picture."

"No," Krisha said, her eyes darkening. She moved toward the doorway to her room. "Forget the shampoo, I'll just wash my hair with soap."

Nicki glanced helplessly at Kim, who sat calmly in bed watching the scene. "It's okay, Krisha," Nicki said, hurrying after her. "Take the shampoo. I didn't mean to upset you."

Krisha stared at Nicki's outstretched arm for a moment, then slowly smiled and accepted the bottle of shampoo. She lifted one shoulder in an elegant shrug. "Sorry. It's just that my passport is six years old and I took a horrible picture and I'm a little ashamed of it. I had braces back then, and an ugly birthmark on my face, and horrible hair—" she shuddered. "I don't show that thing to anyone unless I absolutely have to."

"Forget it," Nicki said, waving her hand in the air. "I won't ask again. But . . . ," Nicki ran and jumped on the bed where Laura was spreading out her beauty lotions and makeup, "I figured out where we might find the bracelet. Has it occurred to anyone that it might be downstairs in the hotel's lost and found? If we get to the lobby before your mother, Laura, we can claim the bracelet before breakfast."

Laura tucked one leg under her and bit her lip. "Do you really think so?" she asked doubtfully.

"It's worth a try," Nicki answered. "So hurry up your beauty regime, Laura, and let's get downstairs. I'm starving!"

"Do we have an item of jewelry in our lost and found? Yes, we do," the girl behind the desk answered crisply. "But it was turned in last week. We have had nothing turned in yesterday or today."

"Thank you," Nicki answered politely. She patted Laura's shoulder. "Don't worry. If it's lost, it still might turn up here. We'll just have to check every morning and every night."

"There is something else we can do," Kim volunteered. "We ought to pray that we find Laura's bracelet. We have been so busy thinking and rushing around that we haven't stopped to pray about this."

Kim was right. Of course they should pray. "We'll do it right now," Nicki said, bowing her head. "I feel bad that we didn't do this sooner."

Nicki, Kim, Meredith, Christine, and Laura bowed their heads for silent prayers, and when she raised her eyes Nicki was surprised to see that Krisha's face wore a look of disbelief. When she felt Nicki's eyes upon her, though, Krisha jerked quickly away.

"It's too bad we didn't know what that other piece of jewelry in the lost and found was," Krisha remarked. "We could have claimed it. Maybe it's something really valuable."

Laura's eyes flashed. "It wouldn't be right to claim something that's not ours," she exclaimed. "Why, that's worse than stealing! That's lying *and* stealing!"

Krisha only shrugged, and Meredith gave Nicki a warning glance. Nicki was beginning to wonder just what kind of girl Krisha was.

At breakfast, Krisha was the perfect guest. She told stories of her travels with her grandfather that kept Mrs. Cushman in stitches, and Nicki had to admit that Krisha's manners were flawless. She seemed to know just what to say to every adult she met, and soon she had the waiter, Mrs. Cushman, and even the busperson charmed.

Maybe Krisha's charm lay in her eyes, Nicki mused—pale green eyes with a splash of blue and fringed with sooty lashes that fluttered expressively. Or maybe it was her bright expression of eager friendliness. Whatever it was, people gravitated to her.

Kim watched Krisha in wonder and amazement, Christine seemed thrilled to be with someone who was older, and even Laura begrudgingly admitted to Nicki that Krisha was pretty. Only Meredith seemed reserved around Krisha, and Nicki suspected that Krisha had made it plain that she didn't like smart people—as if being smart somehow made a person a questionable friend.

"Where are we going today, Mrs. C?" Krisha asked in her warm Southern drawl as she poured Laura's mother another cup of tea. "My grandfather wants to be on his own this morning, so I'm free to go with you all."

Mrs. Cushman beamed as if Queen Elizabeth herself had agreed to join them. "Well," she said, spooning sugar into her tea, "I thought we'd start at Harrods. There's no store in the world quite like it, you know. Then

I thought maybe we'd take a cruise down the River Thames, and perhaps take in a show at the theater tonight."

"Sounds wonderful," Krisha said, sipping her tea. "I love Harrods."

Krisha launched into a story about shopping in London, unaware that her grandfather was approaching from the lobby. He tiptoed up to Krisha from behind, put his hands on her shoulders, and quickly bent to kiss her cheek. Krisha's eyes flew open in surprise, and she pulled away from him as if startled.

No, more than startled, Nicki thought. *She looks like she's scared to death.*

Mr. Smithson put his hand to his chest as if to apologize, then spoke to his granddaughter with a rapid flurry of hand signals. Her face reddening, Krisha answered, then timidly waved goodbye.

"He surprised me," she said, laughing stiffly. "I didn't know who was grabbing me."

"He's a charming man," Mrs. Cushman said, removing her napkin from her lap. "You must ask him to join us for dinner. But now, girls, Harrods is waiting!"

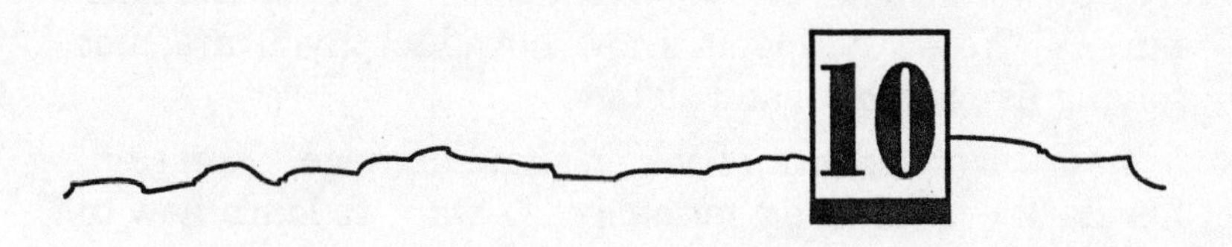

Harrods was the biggest, most extravagant department store Nicki had ever seen. Like an entire shopping city in one building, it offered restaurants, a ticket agency, a bank, a bookstore, and a beauty salon, plus floors of clothes, home furnishings, and everything else anyone could imagine.

"Let's split up, but stay with at least one other person," Mrs. Cushman told them. "We'll meet right back here at this door at noon for lunch. If you're not here, I'll call the police, so don't be late. Agreed?"

After Mrs. Cushman had left, Krisha announced to the other girls that she wanted to shop alone. "Don't take it personally, kids," she said, adjusting the strap of her oversized purse. "But I think I can cover more territory alone. I've got money to spend, and it's burning a hole in my bag!"

She left before any of them could protest, and Laura put her hand on Nicki's arm. "Let her go, Nick," Laura said. "You know I really liked her at first, but she's beginning to wear on me a little. This morning she acted like she knew my mother better than I did! And when Mama finds out I lost that bracelet," Laura added sadly, "she will probably like Krisha better than me."

Nicki patted Laura's hand sympathetically. "It will work out, you'll see," she said, nodding. She looked around at her friends. "Well, what do you want to see?"

"I've got a shopping list from everyone in my family," Christine said, pulling a long sheet of paper from her purse. "You guys don't know how lucky you are, not having five brothers and sisters."

"I want to buy a book on sign language," Kim said, her dark eyes shining seriously. "I want to learn how to talk to Mr. Smithson."

"I want to see the latest fashions," Laura said. "High fashion nearly always comes to London before it comes to Florida."

Laura, Kim, and Christine headed off to look at books and formal wear ("Just to dream," Christine said, "in case we meet the Queen"), so Nicki and Meredith were left alone on the lower floor.

"I don't have any money to spend here, so I don't care what we look at," Meredith said, shrugging her bony shoulder. "What do you want to do?"

"It doesn't matter to me," Nicki said, then she snapped her fingers. "Yes, it does! Let's go to the jewelry counter and see how much a bracelet like Laura's is worth. It may not help us at all, but maybe it'll give us a clue as to why someone would want to steal it."

The jewelry display was large and extravagant, and Nicki and Meredith had a hard time even finding a bracelet as simple as Laura's. Finally, in a small display case, Meredith spied a single gold and diamond tennis bracelet.

"Can you see the price tag?" Nicki said, looking over Meredith's shoulder.

"I can just make it out," Meredith said, peering into the glass. "I think it says twenty pounds."

"Twenty pounds? Why that's only about forty dollars!" Nicki made a face. "That's not exactly a great haul for a crook."

"Can I help you girls?" A tall, thin-faced woman in a tailored plum suit stood behind the case. It was obvious from her tone that she didn't want to waste much time with two American teenagers window-shopping for costume jewelry.

"We like this bracelet," Nicki said, pointing to the tennis bracelet, "but those aren't real diamonds, are they? We want to see a bracelet with *real* stones."

"Those are real zircons," the saleslady answered, her nostrils flaring slightly. "The diamond jewelry is not on this floor. You'll find it upstairs, and I can tell you now that you won't find anything like this up there for less than fifteen hundred pounds."

"Three thousand dollars!" Nicki let out a long, low whistle.

"Well, actually it'd be two thousand six hundred and eighty-five dollars at the current exchange rate," Meredith said, figuring the price in her head. "Still too expensive for us."

Meredith turned to leave, then suddenly she grabbed Nicki's arm. "Guess who else is shopping here in the costume jewelry department?" she whispered. "Miss Hospitality herself. Krisha is over there, hiding behind that display of scarves."

"Why would she hide from us?" Nicki asked, pausing to thank the sales clerk. When she turned and looked, there was no sign of Krisha.

"She saw me, and she knew that I saw her, so she ducked behind the scarves," Meredith said. "Honestly, is she that ashamed to be seen with us? If she wants to act like an adult, why doesn't she just hang around with Mrs. Cushman?"

"She'd like to," Nicki answered, giggling. "But Mrs. C. thinks Krisha is a child, just like Krisha thinks *we're* mere babies." She shrugged. "If she wants to shop alone, there's nothing we can do to stop her."

None of the girls bought anything except Kim, who found a book called *Sign Language Is Simple* in the Harrods bookstore. "It has diagrams and everything," she said, her cheeks glowing with excitement. "I shall begin to learn right away."

When she finally joined their group, Krisha's arm was burdened with a large Harrods shopping bag. She steadfastly refused to show the girls what she had bought. "It's all boring stuff," she said, "underwear, socks, stockings, and a hair brush. Nothing thrilling. I just came to tell you that I'll meet you back at the hotel. I promised my grandfather I'd have lunch with him today."

"I wish you had mentioned it earlier," Mrs. Cushman said, her face registering sincere disappointment. "We could have invited your grandfather for lunch."

"It's all right," Krisha said. "He's kind of a loner. Anyway, I'll catch a cab or ride the tube to the hotel and meet you all there later."

"All right, dear," Mrs. Cushman said, looking faintly worried as Krisha set off through the crowds inside Harrods. "We'll meet you at the hotel in a couple of hours."

When the girls returned to the hotel, Krisha was waiting for them in her room. She stopped filing her nails long enough to give them a quick glance. "There goes my peace and quiet," she said when the girls came in. "The quintuplets are back."

"Look," Meredith snapped, her eyes flashing, "if

you don't want to stay with us you can go find your grandfather."

Krisha threw up her hands. "Forget it y'all, I was just teasing," she said with an easy laugh. "Don't be so sensitive."

Muttering, Meredith went to her room, and Kim and Nicki followed. Nicki sat on her bed and kicked off her shoes. They had done a lot of walking this morning, and it felt good to wriggle her toes. Kim sat Indian-style on her bed and began reading *Sign Language Is Simple.*

"Mom said we should meet her downstairs in half an hour," Laura announced, sticking her head into Nicki's room. "I'm going to brush my teeth and curl my hair."

"I'm going to take a nap," Christine called, curling up on her bed with her pillow. "Wake me as you're going out the door."

"I'd like to watch some television if it won't bother you, Kim," Meredith said, lifting the television remote control from the desk. She pressed a few buttons, but the picture did not come on.

"Wait a minute, and I'll get the remote from the other room," Nicki said, shuffling toward Krisha, Christine, and Laura's room. "Maybe the batteries are low in ours."

The other remote lay on the table next to Krisha's bed, and Nicki tiptoed past Christine as she reached for it. Just as her hand was about to touch it, however, a zinging pain shot through her right toe.

"Ouch!" Nicki cried, grabbing her foot. She hopped on one foot, then sat on Krisha's bed to examine her injury more closely. In the center of her big toe, through the sock, a long silver sewing needle was partially embedded.

"How'd you do that?" Christine asked, sitting up.

"I don't know," Nicki muttered through clenched

teeth. "It must have been in the carpet, and I sort of walked into it. Pull it out, will you, Christine?"

"No way," Christine answered, hugging her pillow and backing away from Nicki. "That's gross."

"Krisha?"

Krisha rolled her eyes, then reached forward and yanked the needle out with one smooth jerk. "Y'all are such babies," she muttered, tossing the needle into a wastebasket.

"How did a needle get into the carpet?" Nicki wondered out loud. "The housekeeper cleaned and vacuumed in here this morning."

"Okay, Nancy Drew, I'll make it easy for you," Krisha answered, her voice dripping with sarcasm. "I sewed a button on my jacket this morning while I was waiting for y'all to come back, okay? No mystery. No big deal."

Nicki shrugged and rubbed her sore toe. The tiny puncture wound wasn't even bleeding. "I wasn't accusing you," she said quietly. "I was just wondering."

"My mother uses dental floss to sew on buttons," Christine added helpfully. "Buttons will stay on forever if you use dental floss."

"Really." Krisha's tone was more than a little sarcastic.

Suddenly a shrill scream sounded from within the bathroom. Nicki and Christine ran to the bathroom door, and Kim and Meredith sprang into the room.

"Laura? Are you okay?" Nicki called through the wooden door.

The door opened slowly, and Laura's eyes were wide and huge in her pale face. In her hand was a plastic toothbrush holder, and there, inside the dull plastic, lay a glittering tennis bracelet.

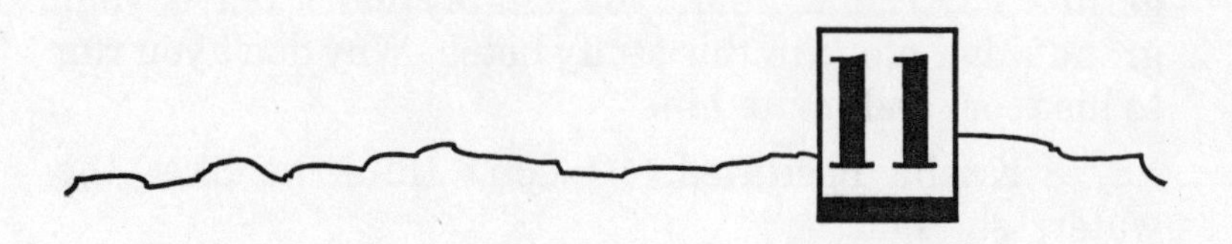

11

You found it," Kim exclaimed. "Our prayers were answered!"

"I don't believe it," Meredith said, her lips pursed suspiciously. "How in the world did your bracelet get inside your toothbrush holder?"

Laura slid the bracelet out of the plastic tube and held it in her shaking fingers. With one hand she brushed tears of relief from her blue eyes. "I don't know," she said, slipping the bracelet around her wrist and struggling to fasten the clasp. "I guess yesterday I was so tired that I wasn't thinking straight. Maybe I put it in here when I was taking a shower or something, and forgot all about it. I feel really stupid."

"You should," Krisha's voice cut across the room. "You made us turn this place upside down, filled the room with dust, practically called everyone from the housekeeper to the concierge a criminal—"

"Maybe we overreacted," Nicki admitted, feeling a little foolish. "But that's how we solve mysteries, step by step. We've solved a lot of problems in the past by taking things one step at a time."

Their discussion was interrupted by a knock on the door. Christine opened it, and Mrs. Cushman came in, the scent of gardenia gently following her. "Girls, I think we should invite Mr. Smithson to accompany us on our cruise this afternoon," she said, clapping her hands together. "Krisha, dear, you simply can't leave your grandfather alone in this stuffy hotel. Why don't you run to his room and invite him."

Krisha hesitated. "I don't think he likes the water," she said.

"You won't know until you ask him," Mrs. Cushman persisted. "I absolutely insist. Go ask him, dear."

"How does one do that?" Meredith asked, raising one eyebrow in her best imitation of *Star Trek's* Mr. Spock. "If a man is deaf, how do you knock on his hotel room door and expect him to answer?"

Krisha stared at Meredith for a minute, then forced a laugh. "I slide a sheet of paper under the door and ask him to contact me," she answered slowly.

"Wow, that's a slow way to reach someone," Christine said. "What if he's watching TV and doesn't go near the door for a long time?"

"You're right, it could take hours to hear from him," Krisha said, smiling at Mrs. Cushman. "I'll put a note under his door, but don't hold things up for him. If he doesn't see it, he wouldn't want us to wait."

"That's fair enough," Mrs. Cushman said. "What room is he in?"

"He's down the hall in room 462," Krisha said. "I'll write the note now."

Krisha moved slowly to the desk and pulled out a sheet of hotel stationery while Laura came out of the bathroom, her bracelet twinkling on her arm. Mrs. Cushman noticed it and smiled. "Your bracelet is lovely, dear," she said, taking Laura's arm tenderly to examine it more closely. "I especially love the tiny inscription on the clasp—they engraved your initials there, did you notice?"

"No, I didn't." Laura and Mrs. Cushman bent their heads over the bracelet, then Mrs. Cushman lifted Laura's arm closer to her eyes.

"That's strange," Mrs. Cushman said. "Laura, honey, take this bracelet off. There's no inscription here at all."

Laura's eyes widened, but she undid the clasp and let the bracelet fall into Mrs. Cushman's outstretched hand. Mrs. Cushman stepped into the bathroom and examined the bracelet closely under the lights.

"This isn't the bracelet I gave you, Laura," she said, her voice registering alarm and disapproval. "This is a cheap imitation. What have you done with *your* tennis bracelet?"

Laura went pale and bit her lip. "I don't know, Mama," she said, shaking her head slowly. "I really thought that was my bracelet."

"She did misplace it yesterday," Nicki said, trying to help Laura out of a bewildering situation. "And we looked everywhere for it, honestly, Mrs. Cushman."

"We even emptied the housekeeper's vacuum cleaner," Christine added.

"And we checked the hotel's lost and found," Meredith pointed out. "They said maybe someone would find it and turn it in later."

"Laura, this is crazy," Mrs. Cushman said, drawing her lips into a tight smile. "Diamond bracelets just don't get up and walk away."

"I know, Mama," Laura said, her voice breaking.

Mrs. Cushman must have realized that Laura was about to cry, because she drew Laura to her in a silent hug. Then she released Laura, pulled her linen jacket together, smoothed her skirt, and took a moment to check her perfectly arranged hair in the bathroom mirror.

"I'm trusting you girls to find that bracelet," she said, turning back to face Laura and Nicki. "I don't want to even *think* about its being gone. Just find it, girls, and find it quickly. If you don't find it—" her eyes were pained, as if she had been wounded, "I guess insurance will cover the loss. But it just won't be the same."

Nicki stepped aside to let Mrs. Cushman pass out of the room, and was surprised to see that Krisha had already gone to deliver the note to her grandfather.

Meredith noticed, too. "Too bad Krisha missed all the excitement," she remarked, giving Nicki a quick, half-sly look.

"Yeah, it's too bad," Christine echoed earnestly.

"We probably need this time without her," Nicki said, sitting on the edge of Krisha's bed. She patted the space beside her. "Come on, Laura, and sit down. Has it occurred to anyone that we now have two bracelets? The diamond bracelet is missing, and the other, a cheap fake, has been substituted."

"What does that mean?" Christine asked, blowing a stray wisp of hair out of her eyes.

"It means Laura didn't lose her bracelet, someone definitely took it," Meredith said flatly, sitting next to Kim on Laura's bed. "And my guess is that the thief is our new roommate."

"Krisha?" Christine's green eyes flared. "No way. She's got money of her own, so why would she take it?"

"How do you know she has money?" Laura asked, sniffling. "My mom has bought everything for her so far."

"She did a lot of shopping at Harrods," Christine said, pointing to Krisha's green shopping bag in the closet. "And once when she opened her purse I saw a wad of traveler's checks just tossed in there. She doesn't need to steal."

"We cannot eliminate the housekeeper or the concierge," Kim said. "As much as I hate to think that either of them would steal, it is possible."

"Tilda or Gregory," Nicki mused, crossing her legs. "How do we find out who did it?"

Laura pointed to Krisha's huge purse. "For starters, we can search through Krisha's things."

"No!" Christine roared, practically falling off her bed. "That's not right. You can't go through someone else's things without their permission. That's snooping."

"Even policemen have to have a search warrant," Meredith pointed out. "So that's out, unless Krisha invites us to take a look."

"What about Gregory?" Nicki asked. "Maybe we could talk to him."

"That couldn't hurt," Meredith said. "Maybe we could even arrange some kind of little test."

"It's all useless," Laura said, her eyes once again filling with tears. "My bracelet is gone, and my mother will never forget this. She may never forgive me."

"Don't give up yet," Nicki said, motioning to Meredith. "Come on, Mere, let's go in the other room and decide what to do. We'll concentrate on the ever-so-charming Gregory first."

"Okay," Meredith said, following Nicki out of the room. "Maybe he's too charming for his own good."

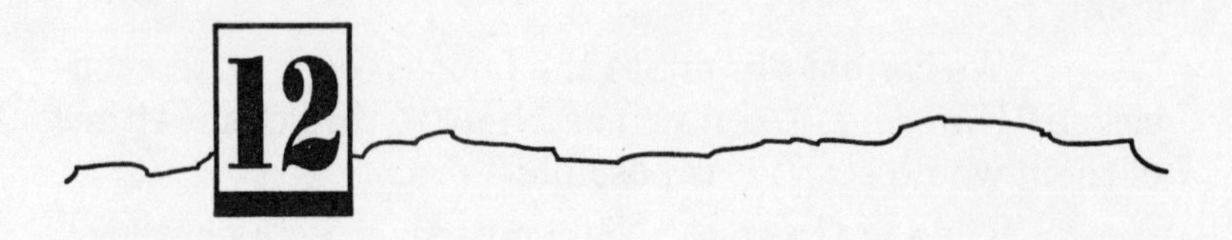

Nicki smoothed her hair and checked her lip gloss before she and Meredith rounded the corner from the elevator to the concierge's desk. Gregory was busy working there, slipping tags onto suitcases in a huge row of luggage.

"Did a tour group come in?" Meredith asked brightly, leading the way to the concierge's desk. She leaned on the desk with her elbows. "You probably don't have time to help us with something."

Gregory straightened up and smoothed the jacket of his uniform. "For lovely ladies, I always have time," he said, his dark eyes dancing. He left the luggage and stood right in front of them. "How can I help you?"

"Well, first we want to know if anything has been turned in for the lost and found since breakfast," Nicki said. "Laura is still missing her diamond bracelet."

"Nothing has come in," Gregory said firmly, his classically handsome features reminding Nicki of a Greek statue. "I checked right before lunch."

"That's okay, but we really don't think it will come in," Meredith said coyly, tracing the designs on the marble counter with her finger. "You see, someone switched an inexpensive copy of the bracelet for the real one. So that means someone stole the real one and tried to cover up the theft, and we want to know how that would be possible. We are, after all, in a secure hotel."

Gregory drew in his chin. "I do not think that would be possible," he said, his voice growing deeper. "The room doors lock as soon as they are closed. Only the hotel staff have access to a master key, and we patrol the corridors regularly. While we do have the occasional break-in, the Hotel Robyns prides itself on its excellent security record."

"This was not a break-in," Nicki said. "Anyone who broke into our room wouldn't have left a fake bracelet. This was someone who was trying desperately to cover his tracks. Maybe it was someone who was afraid of losing her job—or *his* job."

Gregory drew in his breath, and his face wore a horrified expression of disapproval. "You can't mean that I—" he stammered.

"You were in our room yesterday when you brought in the flowers," Meredith pointed out fearlessly. "And we didn't order those flowers, you brought them in on your own."

"As a simple act of thoughtfulness and service," Gregory sputtered. "Really, ladies, I think you have gone too far—"

"I'd be interested to know if the hotel has a record of jewel thefts," Nicki said. "Can we ask the manager?"

"You can, but he's not in now," Gregory replied firmly. "And I've had enough of this conversation. If you want to accuse me, do it now. If you want to file a police report, I will summon an officer for you. But if I cannot help you, I have work to do."

"We're not accusing you," Nicki answered softly. "We're just trying to find out what happened."

"Thank you," Meredith said. She and Nicki turned to walk away, then Meredith caught Nicki's eye. "Step two," she mouthed silently, and then with a quick motion, she allowed a twenty-pound note to fall noiselessly from her pocket and flutter to the floor.

She and Nicki had gone no further than five steps when they heard a voice behind them. "Ladies," Gregory called, holding the money in the air. "I believe one of you dropped this."

"Why, thank you very much," Nicki answered, smiling broadly as she retrieved the note. "Twenty pounds is almost forty dollars—we couldn't afford to lose that!"

She and Meredith thanked Gregory again, then stepped into the elevator.

When the doors had closed and the elevator began its smooth ascent, Nicki handed the money back to Meredith. "He passed the honesty test," she said simply. "He didn't have to return the money you dropped, but he did, even after we insulted him and practically called him a thief."

"He did seem outraged that we made the accusation," Meredith said, reaching into her pocket and pulling out her black notebook. She pulled her handy pencil out of its holder and scratched some notes on a page. "And did you notice that Gregory offered to call the police, but he didn't let us talk to the manager."

"Maybe the manager really was out," Nicki said. "He could have been telling the truth. Anyway, he seemed so shocked by the whole thing that he wasn't thinking very clearly."

"But he thought clearly enough to return our money," Meredith said. "That shows that honesty comes naturally to him. If he were really a thief, he'd just pocket the twenty pounds and not think a thing about it."

"Unless he *knew* we were giving him an honesty test," Nicki pointed out. The elevator doors slid open. "Then he knew he had to return our money, or we'd have him for stealing two things."

"All things considered, I think he passed the test," Meredith said, stepping out into the hall. "I think we can report that Gregory should be scratched off the suspect list."

"Which leaves the housekeeper, and Krisha," Nicki said, absently counting the doors until they reached their room. From inside room 458 she heard the chink of dishes—someone eating lunch from room service. Room 460 had the television turned up loud, and a telephone rang twice in room 462.

"So how do we tell the others about our list of suspects with Krisha sitting right there?" Nicki asked Meredith.

When they reached their room, Nicki rapped gently on the door. Laura opened it and squealed in excitement when she saw Nicki and Meredith.

"Guess what?" she said, pulling Nicki inside the room. "Gregory didn't do it, did he? Well, we know who did!"

"Who?" Meredith demanded, looking around the room. "And how do you know?"

Krisha gave Nicki a lopsided grin. "When I was out earlier this morning, I saw Tilda cleaning rooms," she said. "I don't know why it didn't strike me until now, but I saw her actually wearing Laura's bracelet."

"We've got to find her," Laura said, her blue eyes blazing. "If we hurry, we can do it before Mama meets us downstairs."

"No, we don't have time," Nicki said, checking her watch. "You don't confront somebody in just ten minutes. Besides, it's two o'clock, and the housekeepers are probably already gone."

"But she's *wearing* my bracelet!" Laura whined. "If we hurry, we don't have to say anything! We'll just go up to her, grab the bracelet, and—"

"What if it's not the right bracelet?" Meredith pointed out. "You'll only embarrass yourself and hurt someone else's reputation."

"Of course it's the right bracelet," Krisha said dryly, munching on a bag of potato chips. "What hotel housekeeper can afford a diamond tennis bracelet?"

"Who would steal an expensive bracelet and then have the nerve to wear it to work where everyone could see her?" Meredith countered. "That doesn't make sense."

"So she's no genius like you," Krisha snapped. "Not everybody is as all-logical as you, Miss Genius."

Nicki glared at Krisha. It wasn't right for the older girl to turn on her new friends, especially not after all they'd done to make her feel at home. What was Krisha's problem?

"Anyway," Krisha said, stuffing her bag of potato chips into the nightstand drawer, "we've got five minutes to meet Mrs. C. And if you're smart, no one will even mention that bracelet."

"Oh yeah?" Meredith snapped. Her bold, black eyes were defiant. "Well, if you must know, Krisha, you're right up there on the list of suspects. Maybe we ought to go through your things."

Krisha lifted an eyebrow. "Be my guest," she replied regally. "Look through anything you like, brave scouts. Just don't get grimy little paw prints on anything."

Krisha grabbed her purse and strode out of the

room, slamming the door as she went.

"I'm sorry, I lost my temper," Meredith said, sinking onto her bed.

"So much for approaching the subject delicately," Nicki said, laughing. "Way to tell her, Meredith."

"Well, she just made me so mad," Meredith said. "She acts like she's better than all of us, like she's doing us a favor by letting us hang around her. And we're the ones who are helping her out! We let her stay with us, she eats with us, she goes everywhere with us—"

"Was she serious about letting us look through her things?" Laura asked, her eyes fastened on Krisha's suitcase. "If my bracelet is in there, could we find it?"

"We can look, but we don't have time now," Nicki said. "If we take time, she could tell your mother what we're up to. If she does that—"

"Let's go," Laura said, grabbing her purse. "My mom doesn't want to hear anything about this. We'll worry about Krisha and Tilda when we get back from the cruise."

"We should go," Nicki said, grabbing her camera and her purse. "Is everybody ready?"

"Just a minute, let me get my souvenir money," Christine said, flinging open her suitcase. She rummaged through her clothes until she found a pair of purple socks, then she reached into one sock and then the other.

"It's not here," she said, her face going pale beneath her freckles. "Ohmigoodness!"

"What's not there?" Nicki called from the door.

"My souvenir money," Christine gasped. "I had nearly a hundred dollars of babysitting money—I mean, over fifty pounds—in here. And it's gone!"

13

Are you sure you didn't lose your money?" Nicki asked as Christine dug frantically through her suitcase.

"I know I didn't lose it," Christine snapped, throwing piles of clothes on her bed. "I took out a ten pound note just this morning before we went shopping, and I distinctly remember stuffing the rest of the money back in my sock."

"Did you lock your suitcase?" Kim asked quietly. "My mother told me to always lock my suitcase if I had money inside."

Christine shook her head. "No, I didn't. I lost the key somehow in all this mess."

"You probably just misplaced your money, too," Laura said, tapping her toe impatiently. "We've got to get downstairs. My mother's waiting, and Krisha's down there with her."

"Maybe Krisha took it," Meredith said.

"Or maybe the housekeeper took it," Nicki suggested.

"Or maybe you just misplaced it because your suitcase is so messy," Laura said, opening the door. "Come on, we'll find it later. If you need money, we'll help you out."

"Oh yeah?" Christine answered, flinging a pile of underwear back into her suitcase. "Are you going to buy souvenirs for Tommy, Torrie, Gaylyn, Stephen, Corey, and my mom and dad? I promised I'd bring them all something, and now I can't bring them anything except maybe a barf bag from the airplane!"

"Jeepers, don't get so upset," Laura answered, moving out into the hall.

Christine grabbed her purse and jacket, but she kept muttering under her breath. Nicki held the door open as Kim and Meredith passed through, but she stopped Christine. "You don't need to worry," Nicki said. "Mrs. Cushman won't let you starve, and I've got enough money to share for munchies and some cheap souvenirs. You'll be okay."

"You don't understand," Christine said, her anger dissolving into tears. "That money was an entire year's babysitting money. I had a big fight with my parents before they'd even let me bring it because they wanted me to save it for my college fund. Mom said I'd waste it on nothing. I promised her I'd bring home really neat stuff. I guess she was right—I'll go home with no money and nothing to show for it. It just makes me so mad!"

Angry tears spilled out of Christine's eyes, and she dashed them away with a defiant gesture. "That's what makes stealing so bad," she went on. "Someone who steals doesn't know or care how hard the other person worked to earn whatever they have. Thieves are just lazy. How can people be that way, Nicki?" Christine clenched her hands into fists. "If Krisha took my money, I'll slap her. If the housekeeper took it, I'll call the police."

"And if you find the money in another sock," Nicki said, closing the door behind them, "you'll feel really sorry for all the things you're saying now."

Mrs. Cushman, Krisha, and Mr. Smithson were downstairs waiting in the lobby when the girls stepped off the elevator. "Finally," Mrs. Cushman breathed, rising to her feet and smiling at Mr. Smithson. "I was about to send a search party for you girls."

"We were held up," Nicki said, smiling carefully at Krisha. "Christine lost something valuable and wanted to find it."

"Well, don't worry, dear, I'm sure it will turn up," Mrs. Cushman said, pulling her soft cashmere sweater around her shoulders. She nodded toward Mr. Smithson. "Look who was coming into the lobby just as I came down! I stopped him, of course, and when Krisha came down she invited him to go with us on our river cruise."

Mr. Smithson must have known that he was the subject of the conversation, because he stood and bowed slightly to the girls. Krisha stood up too, and Nicki thought she seemed a little disgruntled. Was she upset because her grandfather was along? Or did she realize they were hinting that she took Christine's missing money? Nicki wasn't sure.

"Well, shall we go?" Mrs. Cushman asked, gesturing toward the door. Mr. Smithson moved his carved walking stick to his right hand and gallantly offered Mrs. Cushman his left arm, which she took with a bit of graceful fussing and blushing. Krisha went out the door behind them, her head down, and Nicki and her friends brought up the rear.

Mr. Smithson led them to Victoria Station, the entrance to the London subway system, and Nicki was delighted that Mrs. Cushman had decided not to call another cab. The subway, or the "tube," as Londoners called it, was the cleanest, busiest place Nicki had ever seen. Thousands of people strode with amazing energy up and down the staircases and escalators and through the tiled tunnels that led to the fast-moving electric trains. It was all Nicki could do to keep up with her friends.

Once inside Victoria Station, they waited a few minutes for a train. When it arrived, they quickly hopped aboard. The train was crowded with commuters, and Nicki found herself standing with Krisha, Meredith, and Mr. Smithson. The other girls and Mrs. Cushman crowded into seats and tried to look comfortable. Nicki had to hide a smile when she noticed how uncomfortable Mrs. Cushman appeared. The subway wasn't her style, but she had followed Mr. Smithson gamely into the tunnels. For a man who was deaf, he certainly had no problem getting around.

"I could ride this train all day and have fun just looking at people," Kim said, trying to cheer up Christine and Laura who sat gloomily next to her. "Just look around us. I've seen Asians, Africans, people from India—"

"I think I've heard about a thousand languages," Meredith added as she held onto a pole for support. "And did you see the papers everyone is reading? London must have a hundred newspapers."

"It seems like it," Krisha said agreeably, smiling at Mrs. Cushman. "But the English do like their newsstands, sweet shops, and—"

"And flowers," Kim added. "I've never seen so many flower boxes. There are geraniums, English ivy, impatiens—"

"Okay, so they like plants," Laura snapped. "Can we cut with the travel report? When do we get there, Mama?"

Mrs. Cushman ducked her head to read the route map above Meredith's head. "I believe the next stop is the Charing Cross Embankment station," she said. "Then I think we walk down to the pier to meet our boat." She shrugged. "I don't know, really, I'm just following Mr.

Smithson. We can always ask someone if we get lost."

"I don't know how they find their way around here," Christine muttered, staring at the floor. "Everything's crowded, they drive on the wrong side of the road, and I haven't seen a straight street yet."

"It's not hard," Krisha said, smiling down at Christine. "Once you learn the tube routes, you can go practically anywhere."

Christine didn't answer, but silently glared up at Krisha, her eyes blazing like emeralds. Nicki was relieved when the train lurched to a stop and the doors opened. "Mind the gap," an electronic voice warned as they stepped from the train to the platform. "Mind the gap."

Nicki sighed. With Christine, Meredith, and Laura mad at Krisha, soon there'd be a gap a mile wide in their hotel room. How could Nicki keep peace *and* help solve the mystery of the disappearing diamonds?

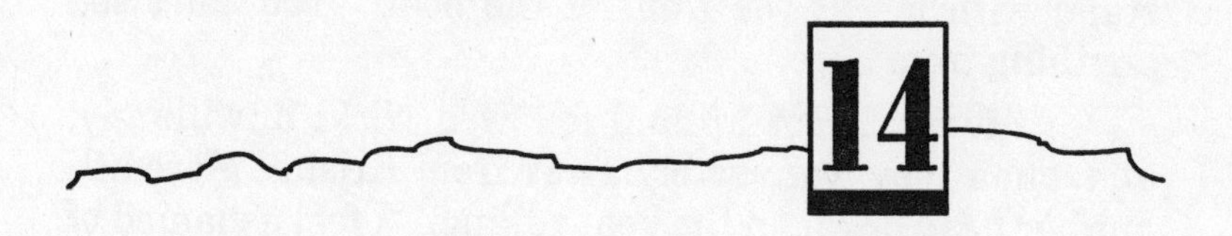

Despite the chilliness between Krisha and the other girls, the riverboat cruise was interesting. "I always thought the name of this river rhymed with *flames*," Christine said, hanging her head out of the boat's large picture window. "I would never have guessed that *Thames* rhymed with *gyms*."

"Explain that if you can, Miss Genius," Krisha remarked in Meredith's direction. "Or is your knowledge of linguistics not that complete?"

"I wouldn't bore you with the details," Meredith answered, looking steadily away from Krisha. "And I'm glad your grandfather can't hear your little remarks. I'm sure he'd love to know what kind of person you really are."

Krisha moved her chair closer to Meredith's. "And what kind of person is that?" she snapped, leaning toward Meredith's face.

Meredith's nostrils flared in anger, and Nicki knew Krisha was heading for trouble. If something wasn't done soon—

"We're about to cross under the famous Tower Bridge," the announcer's scratchy voice called over the public-address system. "It is painted blue because blue was Queen Victoria's favorite color. Many people think this is the London Bridge, but it is not."

"Come see this, Meredith," Nicki said, standing

and literally pulling Meredith away from Krisha. "Come stand with me at the front of the boat. You can't see anything from here."

Meredith got up and followed Nicki unwillingly, and when they were safely away from Krisha, Meredith put her head down on the boat railing. "I feel ashamed of myself because she makes me so mad," Meredith muttered, beating the railing with her fist. "I mean, I'm not a hateful person or anything, and I tried to be nice to her at first. But Nicki, she's making everyone miserable. Don't you think we could ask her to get out of our room? Nobody's having a good time on this trip."

"Mrs. Cushman invited her, and she's as sweet as sugar to Mrs. Cushman," Nicki pointed out. "We'd seem like rude brats if we asked Laura's mom to kick Krisha out."

"What if she's the one stealing from us?" Meredith said. "What if she took Christine's money and Laura's bracelet?"

"Why would she do that?" Nicki asked. "You saw the stuff she bought at Harrods. She has plenty of money, so why would she take Christine's? And she told us we could look through her stuff, which means she doesn't have the bracelet."

"Maybe she gave it to her grandfather," Meredith said, glancing back at the old gentleman.

"Ha!" Nicki laughed. "I've never seen a sweeter or more harmless man in my life. He looks more like an English professor than a thief."

"He's a mechanic, remember?" Meredith said, her forehead wrinkling in a frown. "Retired."

"Whatever," Nicki shrugged. "Anyway, he's deaf. We can't accuse him or talk to him because we don't know sign language and apparently he doesn't read lips very well. Besides, he hasn't been around enough to do anything."

"Yeah, he certainly doesn't spend much time with his granddaughter," Meredith laughed. "Maybe he knows what a brat she is."

Meredith was smiling when she left Nicki and stood next to Kim, but Nicki stood at the rail and watched Krisha and her grandfather. Mr. Smithson's eyes were alert, taking in every sight along the waterfront even though he couldn't hear the tour guide's description, and occasionally he would tug on Krisha's sleeve and gesture abruptly. Krisha would then sign an answer, and Nicki guessed that he was asking about the sights as they went by.

"Over to your right, ladies and gentlemen, is the Royal Naval College, whose buildings often double for Buckingham Palace in Hollywood movies," the tour guide announced. "The Royal Naval College occupies the site of a royal palace, the Palace of Placentia, which was built in the fifteenth century. Here Henry the Eighth and his daughters, Mary and Elizabeth, were born, and Edward the Sixth died here."

"Isn't it strange," Laura said, coming to stand at the rail with Nicki, "that the British talk about the kings and queens who have been dead for hundreds of years as if they died yesterday? We don't go around talking about George Washington all the time."

"I guess we don't have the same sense of history that they do because we haven't been around nearly as long," Nicki said. "But then again, my ancestors came from Europe, so I guess their history is my history, too."

"I don't know where my ancestors came from except Georgia," Laura admitted, looking out over the muddy river water. "But maybe my great-great-ancestors sailed on this very river. Maybe one of them docked near this port, or maybe one of them was hanged on the execution dock we passed! That's right, hanged because he or she was loyal to the queen in a time of tyranny, and someone was trying to overthrow the throne, and—"

Nicki snapped her fingers in front of Laura's face. "Come back to earth, Laura," she said. "The boat's stopping here and I'm dying of thirst. Come with me for a Coke, will you?"

Laura snapped out of her reverie and nodded gamely. She followed Nicki down the boat's gangplank to a small food stand where people were milling about on the waterfront, enjoying the late afternoon sun.

Nicki and Laura had just ordered Cokes when they heard frantic footsteps approaching. Kim, Meredith, and Christine came running up, their eyes wide with unspoken news. "Hurry," Christine said, pausing to catch her breath. "We saw her and she's got it on. We can do something now."

"Saw who?" Laura asked, paying the clerk for the Cokes. "And she's got *what* on?"

"Your bracelet," Kim said, nodding fervently. "Tilda is here—sitting down on the dock with a man, and she's wearing the bracelet."

Nicki took the Coke Laura offered her and drank a quick swig. "Where's Krisha?" she asked, looking around. "And where are Mr. Smithson and Mrs. C.?"

"They stayed on the boat," Christine explained. "Mrs. Cushman wanted to talk to Mr. Smithson, and Krisha had to stay and interpret for her."

Nicki pursed her lips. Maybe it was best to talk to Tilda without Krisha being there. After all, it was Krisha who first insisted that the housekeeper was the thief. And Krisha had been so mean lately, there was no telling what she would say.

"Okay, let's go make sure it's really Tilda," she said, tossing her cup into a litter bin. "Then we'll make sure it's really Laura's bracelet. Remember, Mrs. C. said Laura's bracelet has her initials engraved on it."

"Who else's could it be?" Christine asked, setting her jaw in a determined line. "Maybe Tilda will confess that she took my money, too."

"Just go easy," Nicki warned as they set off. "We're going to ask a few questions, not make her walk the plank."

Nicki was hoping that Christine and the others had mistaken someone else for the housekeeper, but there was no mistaking Tilda's curly blonde hair and rosy cheeks. She was wearing a leather skirt and a soft pink sweater, and her hands were resting on the arm of the man Nicki assumed was her date. He was attractive and seemed to be about twenty-five or so.

Nicki and her friends stopped about five steps from the table where Tilda sat. Christine cleared her throat noisily, and Tilda looked up. At first she stared at them blankly, then Nicki saw the spark of recognition in her eyes.

"It's the American girls from the 'otel," she told her companion, who smiled at them with a glimmer of curiosity in his eye. "Six of 'em in two adjoining rooms."

"We thought we recognized you," Nicki said, smiling. "I hope we haven't been leaving the room in too big a mess."

"I've seen worse," Tilda answered. She paused to take a sip from the glass in front of her, and Nicki noticed that she made no move to hide or disguise the glittering tennis bracelet that dangled from her slender wrist.

"You girls out seeing the sights?" Tilda's boyfriend asked. "The river cruise," Meredith said, her eyes glued to the bracelet. "We're learning a lot."

"What a pretty bracelet," Christine blurted out abruptly. Nicki winced. Subtlety was not Christine's strong point.

"May I see it?" Christine asked.

Tilda gave her boyfriend a puzzled look, then held her arm out for them to take a look. "My boyfriend, George—" she nodded at the young man across from her, and he nodded to the girls, "'e gave this to me yesterday," she said, smiling politely. "'Twas my birthday, you know. Isn't it lovely?"

Christine reached eagerly for Tilda's hand, and slid the bracelet around so they could all see the clasp. It was a simple gold hook without ornamentation or an inscription of any kind.

"Oh," Christine said, her voice falling in disappointment. "I mean, yes, it's lovely."

"It is," Nicki agreed. "Happy birthday a day late, Tilda. I hope you had a great day."

"Thank you," Tilda replied.

"Oh, I almost hate to mention this," Christine asked, lifting her eyes again to Tilda's, "but I lost some money this morning. You didn't see it on the floor, did you?"

Tilda shook her head. "If I find anything in a room, I always put it on the desk," she said. "But I don't remember finding anything today. In fact," she snapped her fingers, "I didn't clean your room at all this morning. I filled in for Nellie on the third floor "

Meredith shuffled her feet uneasily. "Well, I guess we'd better get back on board the boat," she said. "I wouldn't want to spend the night down here on the river!"

Tilda and George laughed politely, and Nicki and the others turned and walked away. They hadn't gone far, though, when Nicki overheard George remark, "An odd breed, American girls. Overly friendly, aren't they?"

If you only knew, Nicki thought to herself. *Our little conversation had nothing at all to do with friendship.*

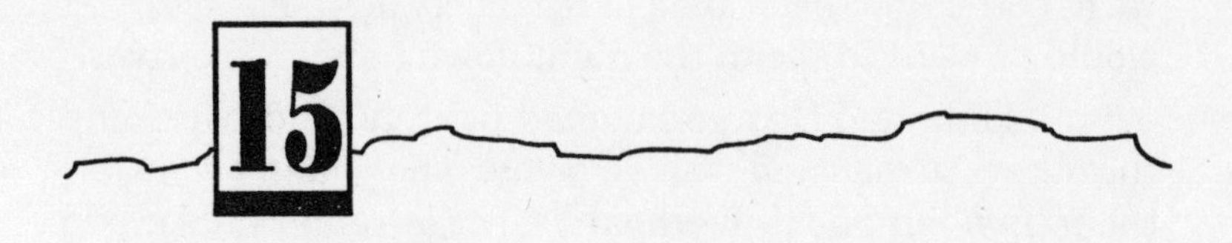

Nicki tossed and turned in bed. They had finished a long, full day, but something wouldn't let Nicki sleep. Twice in two days she and her friends had been victimized by a thief, and it was beginning to look as though their new friend Krisha was nothing but a common crook. To make matters worse, whether she was a thief or not, Krisha certainly wasn't going to win the Miss Congeniality award. She had been hostile to Meredith all day, and even sweet Kim was beginning to eye Krisha with suspicion.

Nicki rolled over and beat her pillow, trying to get comfortable. It was too quiet in their hotel room, that was the problem. At home she had a ceiling fan that creaked and whirred all night, but here there was nothing but silence and the occasional muffled sound of people walking by in the hall and slamming the doors to their rooms.

Kim and Meredith had no trouble falling asleep. Kim had timidly asked that they leave the bathroom light on and the door cracked, and though she didn't want to admit it, Nicki felt better with that tiny stream of light coming into their room.

She sat up in bed and hugged her knees, looking at her friends. Kim slept flat on her back, her pretty porcelain complexion looking like a china doll's, and Meredith slept scrunched in a ball, her head nearly touching her knees. Nicki wondered if turning on the television would wake them—there was nothing else to do. She certainly wasn't sleepy.

Nicki tensed when a muffled sound from the other room caught her attention. She couldn't see into the room where Krisha, Christine, and Laura were sleeping, but she could hear the faint sound of someone moving around in the darkness. Nicki squinted, trying to see through the open door that joined the two rooms. Had someone come in? Had the girls forgotten to lock the dead bolt on their door?

Nicki slipped silently off her bed and padded across the floor until she was in the doorway. A tiny sliver of light shone from the courtyard lamp through the curtains, and she saw Krisha asleep in her bed. Laura, too, lay sleeping, and against the wall a quiet mound was shadowed on Christine's bed.

Nicki stiffened as she heard a thump from the closet. If the girls were in their beds, who was in the closet?

Something jerked on the edge of her gown, and Nicki clapped her own hand across her mouth to smother her scream. "Shh, it's me," a voice whispered, and Nicki looked down and recognized the glint of Christine's red hair.

"Christine?" she asked, squatting to where Christine sat on the floor near the closet door. "What are you doing? And who's in your bed?"

"No one, that's just a pile of clothes," Christine said, tugging on a suitcase in the closet. "I didn't want to wake anyone. Help me, Nicki. Here—hold my pocket flashlight."

Nicki took the flashlight Christine handed her and shone it into the closet. "What are you doing?" she asked.

Christine's actions became clearer when Nicki realized the suitcase Christine was opening was Krisha's. "You said it wasn't right to go through her stuff," Nicki said, putting her hand on the suitcase lid. "We decided that was wrong."

"That was before she took my money," Christine answered, her green eyes glinting in the semi-darkness. "She told us to go ahead and look, didn't she? I need my fifty pounds, Nicki. I'm not going to spend the rest of the week begging money from you guys. I know my money's here somewhere, and Laura's bracelet, too. I'll bet anything that our stuff is in Krisha's suitcase."

"I don't know about this," Nicki said, moving her hand so Christine could lift the lid. "If she said you could look, then why are you sneaking around and doing it when she's asleep? Why don't you wake her up and ask if you can look?"

Christine paused. "You think I should?"

"I guess so." Nicki nodded. "Yeah, I do."

"Okay." Christine lifted her chin and stood up While Nicki watched, Christine walked to Krisha's bed and gently shook the older girl's shoulder.

"I'll leave," Krisha mumbled in her sleep. "You watch me. You'll never find me."

"What's she talking about?" Christine said, her voice breaking out of the whisper. "I think she's talking in her sleep, Nicki. Come here, and maybe we can carry on a conversation."

Nicki stood and came closer, and Christine bent over Krisha and began to whisper in a soft, spooky voice. "Krisha, this is the voice of your conscience," Christine said, her voice rising and falling smoothly. "Tell me the truth. What did you do with the things you took? Where's the money? Where's the bracelet?"

Krisha's eyes flew open and her lips tightened. "What are you doing?" she asked, her voice ringing clearly through the room. "Is this some kind of kiddie trick?"

"Uh, no," Christine stammered, pulling away. "We were just doing another search of the room for the missing things and we wanted to—"

Krisha sat up and turned on the bedside lamp. In one glance she spied her suitcase lying on the floor. "You wanted to look through my suitcase, is that it?" she asked, turning to Christine with an irritated look. "I told you to go ahead. You didn't have to wake me up."

She snapped off the light with a quick motion and punched her pillow. Christine and Nicki faced each other in the dark.

"Well, I guess we have permission," Nicki said, shining the flashlight on Christine's face.

"I guess we do," Christine answered flatly. "So let's look and see what we find."

They found nothing. No bracelet, no money. They not only looked through Krisha's suitcase ("Two pairs of shoes, two pairs of socks, two bras, one jacket, three sweaters, a cotton dress, and five pairs of underwear," Christine remarked. "She sure travels light, doesn't she?"), but they also checked through the huge purse Krisha carried everywhere. In Krisha's wallet were three twenty-pound notes and a fistful of change. The purse also contained a hairbrush, a makeup kit, and her passport.

Nicki held Krisha's blue American passport in her hand and giggled.

"What's so funny?" Christine whispered, replacing things in Krisha's suitcase.

"This passport," Nicki said. "Krisha was too embarrassed about her picture to let me see it. She got defensive and mad when I teased her about it."

"Oh, let's look at it," Christine said, reaching eagerly for her flashlight. "Put it under the light here, Nicki."

Nicki opened the passport and turned it sideways to look at the first page where the picture and personal information were listed. The small color photograph made both Nicki and Christine gasp.

"This doesn't look anything like Krisha," Nicki whispered. "Unless she's changed her hair color—"

"Her nose, her lips, and her teeth," Christine added. "This isn't Krisha, Nicki."

"She said her passport was really old and she didn't look like her picture," Nicki said, remembering Krisha's words. "But according to what's written here, this passport was issued from Miami in August a year ago."

"It says this is Krisha Peterson's passport," Christine said, pointing to the typed letters.

"But it also says Krisha Peterson was born on October 14, 1972," Nicki added. "That would make the girl in this picture twenty years old when the picture was taken." Nicki tapped the photograph. "This girl looks twenty, but the Krisha we know doesn't."

Nicki flipped through the pages of the passport. On page two, Krisha Peterson had signed her name, and on the following pages it was obvious that she had traveled to many foreign countries. "Look here," Nicki said, flipping through the pages and pointing to the stamped entries, "she's been to South Korea and Australia, Taiwan and Hong Kong, Israel and Britain."

"Wow," Christine breathed, her eyes glowing in the dim beam of the flashlight. "She really gets around."

"Or does she?" Nicki whispered. She turned back to the first page of the passport and stared at the photograph. There was nothing in the picture that resembled

Krisha. She even had the feeling that if the photograph could speak, it would speak in an entirely different voice than Krisha's.

"Something strange is going on here," Nicki said, closing the passport and sliding it back into Krisha's purse. "Don't say anything about it to the others, okay? Especially don't say anything to Krisha."

"Okay," Christine whispered, putting Krisha's purse next to the desk where they had found it. "But we still didn't find the bracelet. And though Krisha has a lot of money in her wallet, there's no way I can prove that any of it was mine."

"I know." Nicki turned the flashlight off and stood up to make her way to bed. "But I'm tired and I can't think anymore. Maybe we'll think of something else in the morning."

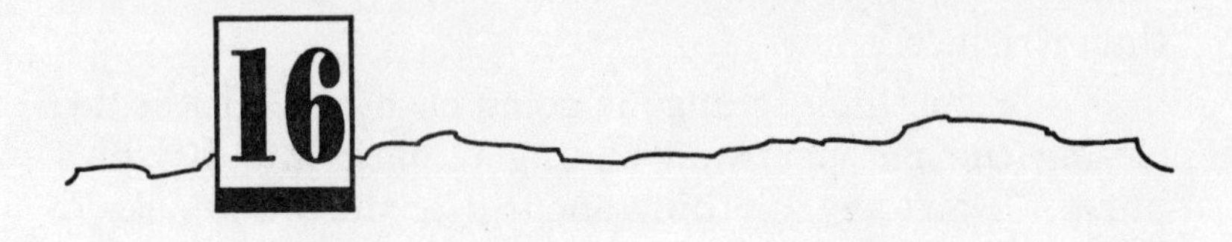

The next morning Nicki overslept. When Meredith finally shook her shoulder and woke her up, Nicki noticed that Krisha and Laura had already gone downstairs for breakfast. "I let you sleep for a while because you couldn't have gotten into the bathroom anyway," Meredith said, running a comb through her damp hair. "But you'd better hustle now. Mrs. C. said she had a busy day planned—I think we're going to the British Museum."

"Oh, yeah," Nicki mumbled, throwing the covers off. "The mummies—that's what you wanted to see, right?"

Meredith grinned. "Right. So hurry up, Nicki. Those bodies are growing older even as we speak."

Nicki stepped into the bathroom and splashed cold water on her face. As the icy water hit her skin, the sleep cloud lifted from her brain and she remembered with startling clarity the photograph in Krisha's passport. Who was that woman and how did she come to be involved with Krisha?

Nicki rubbed her face dry with a clean towel. Soon she'd find the answers she wanted.

Nicki and Meredith were the last two down, and they were surprised to find Mrs. Cushman, Mr. Smithson,

Krisha, Kim, Laura, and Christine already halfway through breakfast. "Mr. Smithson has decided to join us today," Mrs. Cushman told Nicki. "Won't it be wonderful to have an escort? He even suggested that we postpone our trip to the museum and visit the Tower of London instead."

Nicki could see disappointment on Meredith's face. "We'll still get to the museum, won't we?" she asked, pulling out her chair and sitting down. "Meredith's dying to see the mummies."

"No pun intended, I hope," Krisha remarked, smiling brightly at Nicki.

"I promise, we'll get to the museum tomorrow," Mrs. Cushman said, rolling her eyes. "Though why you'd want to spend a day in that dusty place is beyond me."

"My grandfather said that the Tower of London is likely to be less crowded today because it's cloudy outside," Krisha explained, casting a quick glance at Mr. Smithson.

"The Tower of London is okay with me," Meredith said, unfolding her napkin. "It's actually a fascinating place. The wall that runs near it was built by the ancient Romans, and the Tower itself was built by William the Conqueror to help secure London after the Norman Conquest of 1066."

"There she goes, the talking encyclopedia," Laura said pleasantly. "Tell us something *interesting*, Meredith."

Meredith shrugged. "Many people were imprisoned, tortured, or executed there," she said. "Lady Jane, who was queen for nine days and executed at age seventeen by her rival, carved her name on a wall. Is that interesting enough for you?"

"How romantic!" Laura breathed.

"How terrible!" Kim interjected.

Mr. Smithson interrupted their conversation by gesturing rapidly to Krisha, who made a face, then responded in sign language. "He wants a running translation of our conversation," she said, when she had finished.

"I wish you would help me with sign language," Kim told Krisha, her dark eyes shining. "I am learning a little from my book, but it would be so much easier if someone would show me the signs."

"It's too hard," Krisha answered, shaking her head. "And I'm always having to translate for Grandpa. It's a pain. Sometimes I wish I didn't speak it at all."

Nicki tilted her head, wondering if Krisha really meant the things she was saying. Could you ever really grow tired of talking to someone you loved?

"My heart goes out to deaf people," Kim went on. "I read that until the sixteenth century, people did not even try to teach deaf people. They thought because deaf people could not hear, they could not think or even dream. But during that time a Spanish holy man proved you could teach deaf children, and soon men were developing sign language as a tool for communication."

"What else have you learned?" Meredith asked, all ears.

Kim smiled. "When you speak sign language, you should say the words aloud and use facial expressions, too."

"It doesn't do any good to speak aloud with my dad—I mean, grandpa," Krisha interrupted. "He's deaf as a post. Sign language isn't cute or some kind of secret code for kids, it's just a fact of life and I'm sick of it." She forced a smile. "So can we talk about something else?"

Kim stirred her bowl of cereal silently and would not look up.

"Okay," Meredith said slowly, watching Kim carefully, "at the Tower of London we'll see several historic buildings and several castle rooms that have been furnished to resemble how they must have looked hundreds of years ago. Of course, most people go to the Tower of London to see the Crown Jewels."

"Jewels?" Christine's eyes glittered with interest. "Like in the Queen's crowns and stuff?"

"Yes," Meredith said, nodding seriously. "Major crowns. In the Tower are kept the crown of Queen Elizabeth the Queen Mother, which holds the humongous Koh-i-Noor diamond; St. Edward's Crown, used only at coronations; and the Imperial State Crown, worn by the monarch at all major state occasions."

"Really!" Mrs. Cushman leaned forward eagerly. "What else?"

Meredith smiled. "The head of the Scepter with the Cross, made for Charles the Second, contains the Star of Africa, a diamond that weighs five hundred thirty carats. It's the largest cut diamond in the world."

"So all these crowns and things are just sitting at the Tower of London?" Christine asked. "Why doesn't the Queen keep them at her palace? They're hers, aren't they?"

"Not really," Nicki said. "I read somewhere that although she can use them, they actually belong to the country. The Queen is a wealthy woman, though, even without the Crown Jewels."

"Well, if we're going to go see these wonderful things, we'd better get ourselves together," Mrs. Cushman said, spreading butter on her breakfast scone. "Eat up, girls, and let's get going. I want to be able to tell the folks at home about this."

As she poured herself a cup of tea, Nicki sneaked

a peak at Mr. Smithson. Krisha had steadily ignored him ever since he asked her to translate the conversation, but he sat and ate in silence as if accustomed to missing out on most of everything. What must it be like, Nicki wondered, to live in a world of total silence?

Mr. Smithson felt her glance and raised his eyes as he sipped his tea. When he put his cup down, his eyes were smiling, and Nicki felt that somehow he understood more than most people, even those with two good ears.

After breakfast, they went back to their rooms to brush their teeth and grab jackets. "Mom said it looks like rain, so if you have a raincoat, bring it," Laura said, rummaging through her suitcase.

"The housekeeper was here early," Nicki observed, noticing that the beds had been made and the garbage cans emptied.

"That's because someone put a 'make up this room' sign on the door," Christine explained. "I saw it as I left for breakfast."

"I did it," Krisha said, picking up her purse and looking through it. "I hate a messy room."

Nicki pulled a nylon windbreaker from her suitcase and tied the arms around her shoulders. "Last one out has to ride up front with the cab driver," she called, laughing.

"Just a minute," Krisha yelled, startling everyone. "Last night when I went to bed I had over sixty pounds in my wallet. Now all the money's gone. Who took it?"

Nicki looked at Christine, her eyes widening. Krisha looked helplessly around the room, then her gaze hardened and fell on Christine. "Hey, I just remembered. Last night you woke me up to look through my stuff I said you could look, not take my money!"

"I didn't take anything," Christine protested. "Ask Nicki. She was with me the entire time. Yeah, we saw the money in your wallet, but Nicki saw me put it back."

Nicki closed her eyes. She did see the money in Krisha's wallet, but did she really see Christine put it back? She couldn't remember. Was it possible that Christine had taken Krisha's money to make up for the money that she lost? No, Christine wouldn't do that.

"Neither of us took your money," Nicki said, nodding confidently. "We just looked through everything 'cause you said we could, then we put everything back."

"Then who took it?" Krisha demanded, glaring at Laura. "You're the only other one in this room!"

Laura's jaw dropped. "Me? I didn't steal anything. I'm a victim, remember? Someone's been stealing from me!"

"They've stolen from you, and Christine, and me," Krisha said, looking now into Nicki's room. She walked through the doorway and glared at Nicki, Kim, and Meredith. "Maybe the criminal's not on our side of the doorway at all. Maybe the crook is one of you three."

"No way," Meredith said flatly. "We wouldn't steal your money, Krisha."

"Oh yeah?" Krisha wagged her finger back and forth, like a scolding teacher. "How do I know your little friend here didn't do it?" She looked directly at Meredith. "Or maybe it was you, you—"

"That's enough," Nicki said, jumping to her feet. Her anger erupted strong and raw. "I won't let you accuse my friends and call them ugly names. I feel responsible because I introduced you to everyone, and ever since you came here, you've been getting nastier and nastier. That's enough, Krisha, or whoever you are."

Krisha's face drained of color and her mouth opened helplessly. "What?" she whispered.

"I said whoever you are," Nicki sputtered. "Chris and I saw your passport, and your face doesn't at all match the picture of Krisha Peterson, the woman in the picture. Something's very wrong with you, and I'd like to know what it is. Tell us now or tell us later, but you're going to tell us the truth for a change."

Krisha turned with a quick snap of her shoulders, snatched her purse, and ran for the door. Before any of them could move to stop her, she was gone, her footsteps echoing down the hall.

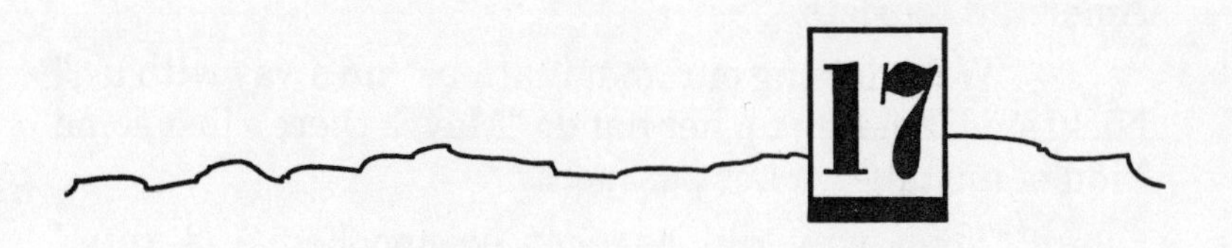

What did you say?" Laura asked.

Meredith whistled in surprise and dashed for her black notebook to jot down the latest developments. "Way to drop a bomb on us," Meredith said, flipping for a blank sheet of paper. "What's this about Krisha's passport? Do you think she's an imposter?"

"I don't know what's going on," Nicki admitted. "All I know is that last night Christine and I checked through her things—with her permission—and we happened to see her passport. It is issued to Krisha Peterson, but the photograph looks nothing like the Krisha we know. And the age is all wrong—the lady in the picture was at least twenty when the passport was issued. Krisha's older than we are, but I don't think she's twenty."

"Wow." Meredith snapped her notebook shut and closed her eyes. "I need to think about this. Is Krisha pretending to be someone else? Could she be a spy? Maybe she's a diplomat's spoiled daughter and she's being pursued by bad guys who want to kidnap her."

"Then who is Mr. Smithson?" Kim asked, coming to sit next to Meredith. "Is he really her grandfather?"

"Maybe he's someone from the Secret Service assigned to protect her," Christine chimed in, coming into Nicki's room. "And when she fell in with us, why, that was the perfect cover for her! No one would expect a diplomat's daughter to be hanging around with a bunch of teenage American tourists."

"We're letting our imaginations run away with us," Nicki said, holding up her hand. "Maybe there's just some kind of mistake on her passport."

"Then why did she get so spooked and run?" Meredith asked, cocking her head to one side. "You left her speechless, Nicki, and I've never seen Krisha speechless."

"And all this time I thought she was just a petty thief," Laura said, giggling. "A pickpocket with a bad attitude. But whoever's been stealing from us—"

"The housekeeper was in here this morning, and Krisha found money missing," Christine interrupted. "And if it's not Tilda who's been taking things, maybe it's another housekeeper. There have to be at least a dozen at a hotel this big."

"Maybe Krisha is some kind of international fugitive," Laura whispered, her cheeks turning pink. "How romantic! How exciting! Maybe that's why she knows sign language—maybe it's not real sign language at all, but some kind of secret code that she uses to communicate with Mr. Smithson—"

"Her bodyguard," Christine added. "And there are hardly any clothes in her suitcase, so she must have had to leave in a hurry. Remember the stuff she bought at Harrods? It was regular stuff—a hairbrush and things you'd probably forget if you were packing to leave town on the run."

"Maybe Mr. Smithson took Laura's stolen bracelet from Krisha and sold it to cover their expenses while they're on the run," Meredith theorized. "That would answer a lot of questions."

"There's only one problem with the bodyguard theory," Nicki said. "Mr. Smithson isn't exactly the bodyguard type. He's older, and with a cane, he's very polite and proper, and he's deaf."

"That doesn't matter," Christine insisted. "Remember the old guy in the *Karate Kid* movies? He knew karate, and he was always jumping in to help Daniel beat off five or six younger guys."

Nicki laughed. "Still, I'd be surprised if Mr. Smithson jumped up and started breaking boards or cement blocks," she said, tossing her head. "But let's keep an eye on him, okay?"

Laura dimpled. "Yeah, he might try to karate chop a guard at the Tower of London," she said, gathering her raincoat and purse.

"This case certainly has developed an interesting twist," Meredith remarked, pulling on her jacket. "If Krisha isn't Krisha Peterson, I guess we'd better find out who she is."

Mrs. Cushman was tapping her foot impatiently by the time the girls arrived downstairs in the lobby. Mr. Smithson sat in a chair behind her, one hand resting on his cane and the other in his lap. He was staring politely into space, pretending not to notice how upset Mrs. Cushman was.

"I was about to call you," she said, her eyes focusing on Laura. "Have you any idea how late you are? Or any idea how hard it is to entertain a man who can't hear a word you say?" She glanced around the group. "Where's Krisha? I was counting on her to interpret for me."

Nicki stepped forward. "Krisha was upset about something and left a while ago," she said, shrugging. "I don't know if she wants to go with us to the Tower of

London."

"You see, Mom," Laura began, but she stopped in mid-sentence when she caught Nicki's warning glance. Nicki had a hard and fast rule about not talking too much, and it was clear from the expression on her face that Laura shouldn't say anything else.

Mrs. Cushman didn't notice Laura's slip, because the hotel door opened and a windblown Krisha rushed into the lobby. "Here she is," Mrs. Cushman said, holding out her arms and drawing Krisha into the group. "My dear, we were about to leave you. You really should tell people where you are going."

Krisha's eyes darted from Nicki to Christine to Meredith. "I wasn't sure I'd be welcome to go with you," she said hesitantly.

Mrs. Cushman looked at Nicki and Laura disapprovingly. "Have you girls had a quarrel? You'd better apologize now, because I'm not touring the Tower with a bunch of gloomy girls."

"It's okay, Krisha," Nicki said slowly and deliberately, looking right into Krisha's eyes. "We won't say anything more about—"

"We'll stand by you," Laura added protectively, raising her eyebrows. She nodded slowly and dramatically. "We *understand.*"

Krisha smiled warily. "Okay," she said, watching the girls closely. "I guess we'll be all right."

"Good," Mrs. Cushman said, beaming. "Let's hail a taxi. I'm dying to see those diamonds!"

The Tower of London was like a huge city itself, a sprawling complex surrounded by a stone wall that reminded Nicki of Cinderella's castle at Disney World, but a thousand times larger and more complex. Bordered on one side by the River Thames, the Tower was surrounded on three sides by modern London. But when she passed through the gate into the centuries-old castle, Nicki had a strange feeling that time here meant nothing. The old castle made her feel very young.

"This first tower on our left is the Bloody Tower," Meredith said, consulting a diagram of the castle.

"Gross," Christine said, shivering. "Why do they call it that?"

"Because, as the story goes, two young princes were lodged in the tower in 1483. Twelve-year-old Edward, the older brother, was supposed to inherit the throne, but their uncle, Richard, Duke of Gloucester, was crowned instead. He was supposed to protect the boys, but he left them in the Tower for a long time and everyone forgot about them until their bones were found buried near the White Tower in 1674."

"What happened?" Nicki gasped.

"No one knows," Meredith said. "Some people speculate that Richard had them killed, but there's no proof." She forced a smile. "But other people have died in the Bloody Tower. Sir Thomas Overbury was poisoned while a prisoner there, and the Eighth Earl of Northumberland—"

"That's enough, Meredith," Mrs. Cushman interrupted, holding up her hand. "Let's dwell on more pleasant things, shall we? Where are the jewels?"

Meredith pointed up the stone walkway. "The Jewel House is straight ahead in the Waterloo Block," she said.

"Let's not waste any time, then," Mrs. Cushman said, leading the way past the Bloody Tower. "Krisha, tell your grandfather that he's in store for a real treat."

Nicki was fascinated by the Tower guards in their bright red uniforms. "Is it true these guards are called Beefeaters?" she asked Meredith as they walked along the stone pathway to the Jewel House. "That's a strange name."

Meredith nodded. "Right. Long ago, servants of a wealthy person were called 'beefeaters' because they were privileged to eat beef when everyone else was too poor. Today the name still sticks, though formally these guards are called Yeoman Warders of the Tower and Yeomen of the Guard. They actually live here in the Tower, and their job is to guard the grounds, the Queen's House, and of course, the jewels."

"Can you imagine living here?" Laura asked, looking around at the huge old buildings. "I'd feel like Sleeping Beauty. I'd want one of those little tower rooms with a fireplace, and I could sit and watch the river—"

"You'd be bored to death," Christine said, interrupting. "And you'd probably be sick of the tourists who come from all over the world to visit this place."

"Look at them now," Kim said, pointing to a group of people who had surrounded a guard outside one of the massive buildings. The guard walked stiff-armed back and forth in front of the door, his eyes never swerving from the space directly in front of him. Though the tourists called to him, laughed at him, and aped his actions, the young man never cracked a smile or frowned in annoyance.

"That guy has more patience than I do," Krisha remarked. "I'd take my rifle and bop one of them over the head if they did that to me."

"I hope you girls never behave like that rowdy bunch," Mrs. Cushman sniffed, frowning in disapproval.

"We won't, Mama," Laura assured her. "Here we

are—the Jewel House."

When they entered the Jewel House through a narrow door, a uniformed guard looked them over carefully and reminded them that photography was not allowed. Nicki craned her neck to see ahead into the room, but a series of glass display cases blocked her view.

The guard motioned toward a pathway marked off by velvet ropes. "I'm going first," Laura called, pulling her mother after her. The others filed in line behind them, and Nicki stared in wonder at the incredible collection of silver and gold swords, bowls and plates, maces and scepters. One display case was filled with ribbons and medals worn by kings and queens of the past, and another held the beribboned gold trumpets used for coronations and royal weddings.

"Look over here," Laura called, motioning toward another huge display case. Inside, on a life-size mannequin, was the official coronation robe used by every English monarch for hundreds of years.

"It's beautiful," Nicki whispered.

"It's so old," Christine said. "You'd think they'd have given the Queen a new outfit. Why did she have to wear this old thing?"

"It's tradition," Nicki said. She read from a sign posted among the coronation regalia. "English kings and queens have used many of these things since the time of King Edward the Confessor."

"We still haven't seen the crowns," Laura complained, looking around. "I mean, this old stuff is neat, but I want to see the jewels."

"Come on then," Krisha said, pointing to another door. "Let's take a look."

The actual crown jewels were housed in a small, windowless room shaped like an octagon. A guard was posted at the entrance, and he nodded briskly at Nicki's group. "Keep the line moving, please," he said firmly, pointing to his right. "If you want to come back for another look, stand behind the rail."

Nicki glanced about curiously. The jewels were inside a glass case shaped a bit like an oversized diamond. They walked steadily past jeweled swords, scepters, and assorted stones until they reached the crowns.

"Isn't it beautiful?" Laura breathed, staring at the Imperial State Crown with its purple velvet lining and circle of bright diamonds.

"That blue stone is the sapphire taken from the ring buried with Edward the Confessor in 1066," Meredith said, reading from her notes.

Christine made a face. "You mean they dug him up?"

Meredith shrugged. "The stone belonged to the kingdom, I guess. That huge ruby in the center was presented to the Black Prince in 1367."

"It's hard to believe those stones are older than our country," Nicki said, laughing. "I mean, that blue sapphire was cut only about a thousand years after Christ died."

"And still seven hundred years before America's Declaration of Independence," Kim added.

"Excuse me, but you'll have to keep the line moving," a guard said. Nicki ducked her head in embarrassment and moved to the next display case.

"This one's even better," Laura breathed, her eyes glowing. "St. Edward's Crown. Look at all that gold!"

"I look better in gold than in silver," Mrs. Cushman remarked absently. "That'd be my choice, if I were queen."

St. Edward's Crown was even larger than the Imperial State Crown. It was solid gold, with huge stones set above the ermine-lined rim, and under the four arches lay a cap of maroon velvet. Atop the four arches was a golden ball rimmed with diamonds, and on top of that, a golden cross set with more precious stones.

"The lower half of this crown," Meredith said, reading from the guidebook she bought, "was made up of a medieval crown thought to be the crown of Edward the Confessor. This crown was fashioned for use at Charles the Second's coronation in 1661. The other monarchs since that date have worn this crown at their coronations."

"So the Prince will wear this when he becomes king?" Christine asked, crinkling her nose. "It'd give me a headache. It must weigh twenty pounds."

"At least that," Meredith said, eyeing the gems carefully.

"Keep moving, please," the guard intoned, and Nicki and the others dutifully stepped to their left, only to find they had completely circled the room.

"If you want to go back, you can slip behind the rail and stay as long as you like," the young guard at the door told Nicki. There was a twinkle in his eye when he smiled at Krisha. "Stay as long as you like, ladies."

Mrs. Cushman slipped under the metal railing and walked back to the display case that housed the crowns. The other girls followed her, and Nicki noticed that Mr. Smithson followed them obediently, like a timid puppy dog.

It's a good thing he can read the printed explanations in the display cases, she thought. *At least he has some idea of what's going on. Kim has the right idea. We really ought to learn to talk to him.*

Nicki was gazing at the Star of Africa diamond in the head of the Scepter with the Cross, when she suddenly became aware of how quiet the room had become. For a few moments the crowd of tourists had thinned, and she and her friends were the only visitors. "Hey, look at this, we're all alone," she quipped, turning to her friends.

Suddenly Christine squealed and Nicki turned completely around. Mr. Smithson, his eyes bulging, clutched his chest with his right hand while his left hand swung his cane helplessly. He staggered forward for a moment, then slumped to the floor.

"Help! Guard!" Nicki screamed, then she ran to loosen Mr. Smithson's tie and collar. The young guard at the door stood by his post and grabbed a telephone from a compartment in the wall, but the guard posted in the back of the room ran over and helped Nicki loosen Mr. Smithson's vest.

"What's wrong with 'im?" the guard asked, looking up at Nicki.

Nicki shook her head and looked at Krisha. "What's wrong with him, Krisha?" she asked. "Does your grandfather have a heart condition or something?"

Krisha's face was as pale as Mr. Smithson's as she shook her head. "I don't know," she protested helplessly, her eyes filling with tears. "I don't know what's happening."

Mrs. Cushman gathered the other girls to her as Nicki and the guard worked furiously on Mr. Smithson. Nicki had just pushed up his left sleeve and was feeling for a pulse when his right hand swung up and clapped the guard on the side of the neck. As Nicki watched in confusion, the guard stared blankly ahead, then slumped over sideways, like a rag doll, his eyes closing as he fell.

Nicki's mind reeled in horror as Mr. Smithson's hand reached for her next.

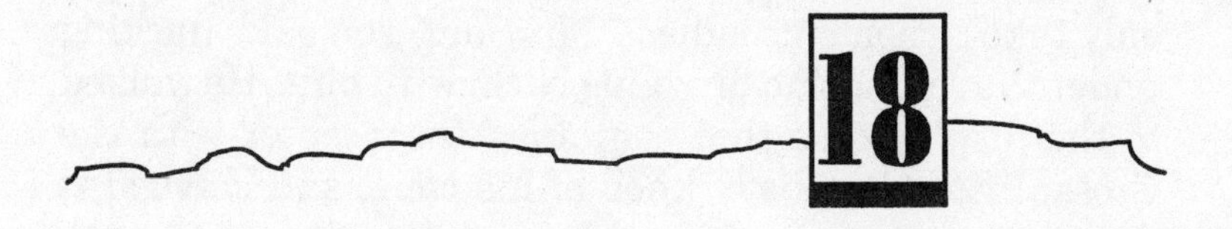

18

In between the fingers of the hand that had seemed so gentle in sign language was something like a giant thumbtack, and Nicki realized that whatever substance was on the point of the needle had knocked the guard out cold—or worse. Mr. Smithson sat up and shook his hand free of the dart, then he caught Nicki by her collar and pulled her close "Don't move, dear, or I'll have to hurt you," Mr. Smithson said, his voice remarkably strong for one who had apparently been having a heart attack a few minutes earlier.

Mr. Smithson stood, and with his right hand still holding Nicki's collar, pulled her in front of him as a shield. His left hand shook the walking stick menacingly toward the young guard at the door. "Put the phone down and lock the door," Mr. Smithson called, his voice clear and commanding. "Do it now, or I'll hurt the girl. You do not know what powers I have, young man."

The young man froze for a second, and Mr. Smithson tapped his cane forcefully against the hard floor. "In the lower half of my cane is a fragile glass vial of a deadly nerve gas," Mr. Smithson called calmly. "If you do not obey, sir, I will smash my cane and we will all die within seconds in this windowless room."

"Please!" Laura squealed from the corner of the room. "Do as he says!"

The guard put down the phone, held his hands up in the air, and quickly moved to lock the door. "This will only take a moment, ladies," Mr. Smithson said, ducking under the railing and dragging Nicki with him. He walked to the display case that contained the Scepter with the Cross, lifted the heavy knob of his cane, and crashed it down upon the glass. In that instant, the glass shattered, alarm bells rang, and Laura screamed.

Mr. Smithson stepped over the broken glass, shifted his cane to the hand that held Nicki, and with his free hand lifted out the Scepter and dashed the lovely golden rod against the floor. Precious diamonds and fragments of gold flew across the room. One object, though, was too heavy to roll—the huge Star of Africa diamond lay at Nicki's feet. Mr. Smithson bent, scooped it up, and placed it in his pocket.

In one quick motion he returned his deadly cane to his right hand and held it aloft. "You're going to let us out of here now," he told the pale-faced guard, "and you're going to go in front of us and clear the way quietly. The gas may not kill a roomful of people once we are out of this place, but it will certainly harm this young girl. Do you understand?"

The guard nodded solemnly and moved to open the door.

"You won't get far dragging a girl," Meredith called. "Why don't you leave Nicki here?"

"Why don't you hush?" Mr. Smithson snapped, then he turned, smiled, and nodded politely to the frightened group. "Thank you, ladies, for your company these last few days," he said gallantly. "I shall never forget our time together."

The guard did as he was told, politely waving back the scores of red-uniformed guards that came rushing to the Jewel House. Nicki felt Mr. Smithson's heart pounding as he pulled her along in front of him, and the smell of his cologne filled her nostrils. It was Royal Copenhagen, the same scent her father wore.

At the thought of her father, Nicki struggled to keep from sobbing. What were her parents doing, safe at home in Florida? Were they thinking of her? Had they remembered to pray for her safety today?

"Please, God," Nicki mumbled, as Mr. Smithson pushed her through the stone halls of the Jewel House. "Please, help me."

They paused in the doorway that led to the courtyard outside. Beyond the guard who led the way, Nicki could see the green of the grass and the movement of tourists who continued about their business as if nothing had gone wrong. Apparently the alarm bells did not ring everywhere on the grounds.

"You will all stay here," Mr. Smithson said, nodding to the helpless guards who watched his every step. "This young girl and I will join the crowd. Please keep your distance."

Mr. Smithson tapped his walking stick on the ground for emphasis and the guards pulled back a few steps. Nicki breathed easier, but Mr. Smithson's arm remained about her shoulders. As he pushed her forward he kept her securely in his grasp, even as they walked down the stairs and out into the sunshine. To anyone watching, Nicki imagined that they looked like an affectionate grandfather and a loyal granddaughter. "Except that I probably look scared to death," Nicki muttered aloud.

"Nothing to be afraid of," Mr. Smithson said, his

dark eyes darting from side to side as they walked toward a large crowd of tourists. "You see, there is safety in numbers, and I plan to be away from here very soon with the prize of a lifetime."

He led her into the crowd of tourists who watched the stiff marching soldier in front of the Waterloo Block, and they casually made their way through the crowd of laughing visitors. Nicki forced herself to look around for a way of escape. The many red-uniformed guards who had been sprinkled through the crowd earlier were gone. Where had they gone? Surely the Tower of London had a better security system than this!

A group of Japanese schoolchildren, all of them wearing white armbands embroidered with the flag of Japan, came trooping by in a group, and Nicki was horrified when Mr. Smithson led her right into the center of them. Their guide was describing the Tower buildings in Japanese, and Nicki saw one of the little girls staring curiously at her. *I must look as pale as a ghost,* Nicki thought. *And even though I'm out here in the open, I can't take a chance on running. What if he breaks that vial of poison gas here among all these little kids?*

When the tour group began to move forward again, Nicki had an idea. She froze in position, and felt Mr. Smithson push her forward. "Move," he said, not unkindly. "We must leave now."

"Just a minute," she said, squinting and crinkling her nose. "I've got to sneeze."

Nicki scrunched up her face as if she were fighting off a whopper of a sneeze, and when the school children had moved on, she thrust her head forward. "Ah-choo!" she yelled, and at the same time she jumped and brought the heel of her tennis shoe squarely down on the arch of Mr. Smithson's foot.

Mr. Smithson lost his dignity and roared an oath, dropping his cane and his hold on Nicki. Nicki bounded away, reaching for the cane, and pulled it safely out of Mr. Smithson's reach.

In an instant, several ordinary-looking men in plain clothes surrounded Mr. Smithson. Still in pain, he raised his hands, lowered his head, and limped over to a bench. It was over. Another thief had tried and failed to steal one of the Crown Jewels.

As Nicki gasped and shuddered in relief, a red-uniformed guard with more decorations than most came over and held his hand out for Mr. Smithson's walking stick. She gave it to him without a word and was surprised when he took it, handed it to another soldier, then stepped back and saluted her.

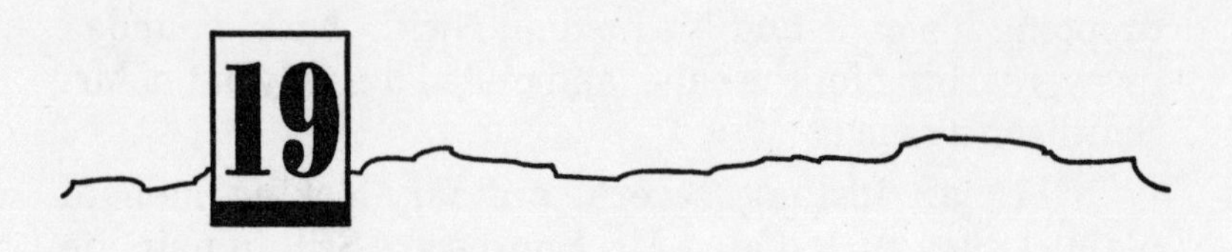

19

Are you okay, honey?" Mrs. Cushman asked Nicki for the tenth time. "I feel just horrible; your parents are going to kill me. They'll never trust me again."

"It's not your fault, and I'm fine," Nicki repeated for about the twentieth time. "Yes, Christine, I was scared, and no, Meredith, I didn't see it coming. And yes, Kim, I remembered to pray."

"I was praying," Kim said earnestly. "The minute Mr. Smithson fell to the floor, I began to pray." She laughed. "I am not sure if I should stop even now."

They were together in a tiny room with green plastered walls near the office of the Yeoman of the Guard. A burly man in plain clothes had brought them to the room, and now they sat on opposite sides of a long wooden table. Mrs. Cushman was wiping perspiration from her brow with a lace handkerchief, Laura was crying silently, and Meredith was scribbling notes in her notebook.

Krisha, however, sat in a corner without saying a word. Finally Nicki turned to the girl. "Are you ready to tell us the truth now?" she asked. "I saw your face in the jewel room, and you were as surprised as we were when Mr. Smithson started talking. You really didn't know he could talk and hear, did you?"

Krisha shook her head.

"How can that be?" Christine asked, crinkling her

nose. "How can you not know something like that about your own grandfather?"

"He isn't her grandfather," Meredith explained. "I thought we established that this morning."

"Then who is Mr. Smithson?" Kim asked.

Krisha shook her head. "I don't know," she said. "I met him the morning I left the United States. My dad is deaf, you see, and I really do speak sign language. Well," she went on, opening her hands and staring steadily at them, "I dropped something and made this off-hand sign that means something like 'darn it' while I was standing in line at the airport. That man—Mr. Smithson—came up and signed that he was deaf. He asked if I would sit next to him on the plane to help him out."

"So you did," Christine said. "And you told us he was your grandfather. Why?"

"Because I was running away from home and I didn't want to explain being on my own," Krisha explained, stuffing her hands into her jacket pockets. "I just wanted to get as far away as I could as fast as I could, so I took my dad's charge card, went to the airport, stole a passport from a lady's purse, and hitched up with the old man. I never dreamed he was conning *me*. All the time I thought I was conning *him*."

"The passport is for Krisha Peterson," Nicki said. "So who are you?"

The girl blinked. "Alana Mitchell," she said simply. "From Atlanta."

"So all that stuff about your grandfather was nothing but a lie," Meredith said. "He's not a retired mechanic, he's—"

"He's not even Duane Smithson," Krisha/Alana shrugged. "I don't know who he is. All the time you thought I was asking him questions, I was usually just telling him that it was a beautiful day or asking him how he slept the night before."

"So you asked to room with us," Laura said. "But how did you think you were going to live in London with no money and no friends?"

Alana shrugged again. "I had a little money," she said, "and I took a bunch of traveler's checks from a lady's bag while everyone was asleep on the plane. But traveler's checks aren't any good unless you're the person who bought them. So then I realized I needed cash, and I—" she ducked her head awkwardly and bit her lip, "—I stole your bracelet, Laura. I took it off your arm while we were on the bus tour. I tried to substitute a cheap one that I bought at Harrods, but I didn't know you'd catch on so quickly."

"Did you take my money?" Christine demanded.

Alana nodded. "I'm sorry. I'll pay it back, I promise."

"But where is the bracelet?" Nicki said. "Did you sell it or give it to Mr. Smithson? We looked everywhere in that room, and it's just not there."

"No, it's here," Alana said. She stood up, slipped off her jacket, and lay it on the wooden table. She ran her finger along the lining for a moment, then lifted the lining to her mouth and ripped the material with her teeth. Through the hole in the lining, she reached in and pulled out the glittering diamond tennis bracelet. "I sewed it into the lining of my jacket," she explained. "You nearly found out, Nicki, when you stepped on my sewing needle."

Alana laid the bracelet on the table in front of Laura and Mrs. Cushman. "Here," she said, lowering her eyelids as if she wanted to see out but not let anyone else see in. "I'm really sorry for taking it. I've been really terrible to all of you. But I figured you'd just use the insurance to replace the bracelet, and you wouldn't really lose anything."

"I'd lose the trust I had placed in my daughter," Mrs. Cushman said softly, "and the trust we placed in you. That trust is priceless."

"What about the money *you* reported stolen?" Christine asked, a soft smile framing her face. "Did someone really steal it?"

"No," Alana shook her head. "I just thought that would throw ya'll off the scent. I tried everything to make you just forget about things and leave everything alone, but you wouldn't." She looked down at the floor. "I even tried to make you feel stupid for acting like detectives, but I was really afraid you'd catch on to what I was doing."

"That's why you didn't like Meredith, isn't it?" Nicki said softly.

"Because she's smart," Alana answered. "I was scared to death that I'd slip or something and she'd figure out that I was nothing but a fake."

"Well, there's one thing we must do immediately," Mrs. Cushman said, rising to her feet. "We're calling Alana's dad in Atlanta and letting him know his daughter is alive and well. You've no idea, young lady, how parents worry about their children. What in the world would make you decide to put your father through such grief?"

A crimson blush rose from Alana's neck until it covered her entire face. "I was mad," she said simply, "because he's getting married again and he won't need me anymore. I didn't think he'd really care much if I left. All he can think about is his new fiancée. So I packed a bag and took off. Dad and I traveled in Europe last summer, so I knew my way around."

"Wait a minute," Laura said, shaking her head. "How can we call Alana's dad? He's deaf."

"I'm sure the police station has a TTD," Alana said. "I'll call and type in the message, and my dad will get it. I'll tell him I'm ready to come home and face everything."

"What happened?" Nicki asked softly. "What made you change your mind about running away?"

Alana's eyes clouded with hazy sadness. "A lot of things, I guess. This morning y'all knew I was a fake, but you didn't tell on me, and you said you understood. I felt like, well, part of a *family*, and suddenly I missed my dad a lot. Then when I saw that man try to steal the diamond, I realized how wrong it all was. That diamond belongs to an entire nation, but he wanted it all to himself and he didn't care who he hurt. I realized that's what I've been doing to my dad—I wanted him all to myself, and I didn't want anyone else to love him. I was hurting everybody by being selfish."

Alana hung her head. "I hurt all of you. Meredith, I'm sorry I was rude to you. Christine, I'm sorry I stole your money. Laura, I'm *so* sorry I took your bracelet. And Kim, you are right to want to learn sign language. I've seen how much deaf people appreciate those who take time to learn how to talk to them. Keep up the good work."

Alana looked at Nicki. "I'm really sorry, Nicki, for everything. You were so nice, and you didn't know that you were bringing a snake into your hotel room."

"I'm sure you're not a snake, Alana," Mrs. Cushman said softly. She walked over and rested her hand on Alana's auburn hair. "You're a precious girl and your dad loves you. We love you, too, and we're going to make sure you get home as soon as this entire episode is cleared up."

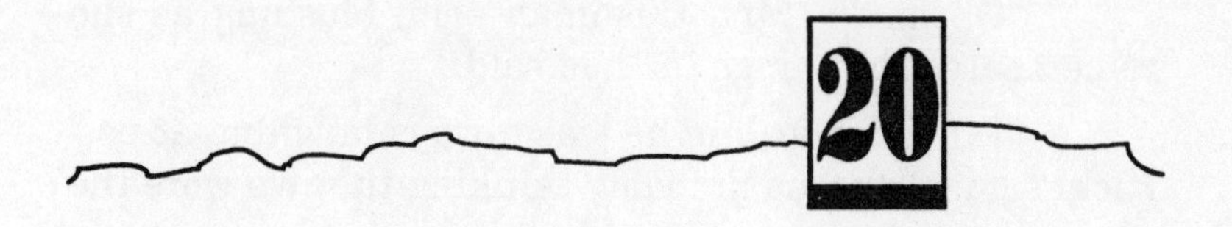

20

I'm Captain Eldridge, and the man you've been traveling with is Hans von Schmittendorf," the captain of the guard told the girls as he came back into the room. He pulled a chair up to their table and waved a thick file in the air. "Von Schmittendorf is an international jewel thief, known and pursued for years. He's smart, quick, and we never know how he'll be traveling. Last year he was spotted in Germany as a priest traveling with a religious group. He slipped away with two million in gold before the authorities could apprehend him."

"This year he was a deaf grandfather traveling with a group of Florida girls," Meredith said, smiling. "Who would have suspected him? We certainly didn't."

"I did notice a few things," Nicki said, "but I didn't think about them. For instance, once I walked by his hotel room and heard the phone ring only once or twice. Why would anyone telephone a deaf man unless he wasn't really deaf? If it had been a wrong number, it would have rung more than twice."

"I noticed that he had clean, smooth hands," Meredith pointed out. "Unusual for a retired bus mechanic."

"I can't believe he heard all that stuff I made up about him," Alana muttered, burying her face in her hands. "I just jabbered away about him, thinking he couldn't hear anything, and he heard every word!"

"Oh, my!" Mrs. Cushman said, blushing as she remembered the things *she* had said.

"I had the feeling he was always laughing at us," Nicki said. "He was probably thinking that we were the perfect cover for what he had in mind."

"Why would he try to steal the Crown Jewels in broad daylight?" Meredith asked. "It would have been impossible for him to escape. No one else has ever been successful, so why would he try?"

"He told us why," Captain Eldridge said. "He's singing like a bird next door. It seems that last year Von Schmittendorf was diagnosed with terminal cancer. In his eyes, he has fulfilled his life's ambition—to successfully steal the Star of Africa diamond."

"But he didn't get away with it," Laura pointed out.

The captain smiled. "He didn't care about getting away with it," he said, pointing at Nicki. "Although he might have gotten away with it if you hadn't thought to trip him up."

"He could never have sold the diamond," Mrs. Cushman pointed out. "No one would buy a famous diamond like that unless it was cut into pieces."

"And no one would dare cut the Star of Africa," Captain Eldridge answered. "No, our man just wanted to be able to say he had stolen it. It was somehow more daring to do it in daylight—sort of the high point of his career, you might say."

"What about the guard?" Nicki asked. "The one who got hit with the dart?"

"Only an anesthetic drug," the captain explained. "He came out of it in a matter of minutes, though he was a bit woozy for a while. And that bit about the deadly gas was all a lark—nothing in that walking stick but wood."

Nicki laughed in relief. "Then I really wasn't in danger?"

The captain shook his head. "Any time you're in the hands of a desperate criminal, you're in danger," he said. "You did a remarkable job."

"It is all a shame," Kim said, looking sadly at the others. "What kind of life did he have if its high point was doing something wrong? How much better he would be if he had done something really good for someone!"

"You've got a point there, young lady," Captain Eldridge said, closing his file. "Well, if you ladies are okay, we'll arrange to have you escorted back to your hotel. Stay near your hotel for the rest of the day, though, because there's talk of a royal reception for you." He grinned as Laura's and Christine's mouths fell open. "It seems Her Majesty the Queen would like to thank you for rescuing a national treasure."

Nicki, Meredith, Kim, Laura, Christine, and Alana all stared at each other in amazement.

"Well, girls," Mrs. Cushman said calmly, standing up and smoothing her skirt, "there's only one thing to do."

"What's that, Mama?" Laura asked.

Mrs. Cushman smiled. "We'll go back and wait for the Queen's call. Then we'll call home and tell *Good Morning America* the news."

"Ohmigoodness," Laura said, clutching Mrs. Cushman's arm. "After that, will you take us to Harrods? I haven't got a thing to wear!"

"We'll have to curtsy, won't we?" Meredith mumbled. "I don't know how."

"I'll meet Prince Andrew," Christine said dreamily, resting her chin in her hand. "And we can fall in love."

Nicki laughed. "You all are too much," she said, her eyes twinkling. "There's nothing to worry about. The Queen is just a regular person."

"Oh, yeah?" Laura asked. "And you're not going to be nervous? I won't know what to say!"

"I might be a little nervous," Nicki said, winking at Alana. "But to break the ice I'll just ask the Queen if she's tried that delicious dish called Shepherd's Poy."

About the Author

Angie Hunt lives in Largo, Florida, with her husband Gary, their two children, and a Chinese Pug named Ike, and Cassie, a calico cat. She recently returned from a trip to London where she visited the Crown Jewels, the Tower of London, and Buckingham Palace. "Don't worry," she says, "the jewels are still there!"

Don't Miss Any of Nicki Holland's Exciting Adventures!

#1: The Case of the Mystery Mark

Strange things are happening at Pine Grove Middle School—vandalism, dog-napping, stolen papers, and threatening notes. Is there a connection between the unusual new girl and the mysterious mark that keeps appearing whenever something goes wrong? Nicki and her best friends want to find out before something terrible happens to one of them!

#2: The Case of the Phantom Friend

Nicki and the girls have found a new friend in Lila Greaves. But someone has threatened Mrs. Greaves and now she could lose everything she loves. The girls have one clue that they hope will lead to something to save Mrs. Greaves—if only they can solve the mystery before it's too late!

#3: The Case of the Teenage Terminator

Christine's brother Tommy is in trouble, but he doesn't seem to realize it. Nicki, Meredith, Christine, Kim, and Laura take on an investigation that pits them against a danger they've never faced before—one that could lead to a life-or-death struggle.

#4: The Case of the Terrified Track Star

Pine Grove's track star, Jeremy Newkirk, has always been afraid of dogs, but now somebody is using that information to scare him out of Saturday's important race. Without Jeremy, Pine Grove will never win! Following a trail of mysterious letters and threatening phone calls, Nicki and her friends are in their own race against time to solve the mystery. Can the girls keep Jeremy's worst nightmare from coming true?

#5: The Case of the Counterfeit Cash

Nicki expected fun and sun in the summer before her eighth grade year—not mysterious strangers and counterfeit cash! Nicki, Meredith, Kim, Christine, and Laura are warned to leave the mystery alone. But when Nicki is threatened, she has to solve the mystery to save her own life!

#6: The Case of the Haunting of Lowell Lanes

Nicki and her friends thought it would be fun to help Meredith's uncle at Lowell Lanes for the summer. But then the lights went out and strange things began to happen. Is Lowell Lanes really haunted? Can Nicki and her friends solve the mystery before Mr. Lowell is driven out of business?

#7: The Case of the Birthday Bracelet

Nicki and her friends thought they were taking a nice vacation trip to London, but strange things begin happening even before the girls arrive at their hotel. And when Laura's diamond birthday bracelet disappears, the search leads Nicki and her friends to more danger than they had bargained for!

#8: The Secret of Cravenhill Castle

Nicki and her friends are thrilled when they receive an invitation to spend a few days at a five-hundred-year-old Irish castle. Shrouded in mystery and fairy legend, the castle is everything they expect, and more! The girls must battle the sea, superstition, and their own fears as they undertake a dangerous search for the legendary treasure of Cravenhill Castle.

#9: The Riddle of Baby Rosalind

Nicki and her friends expected a normal flight home from Ireland until Laura meets a woman in the airport and offers to watch her baby. When the woman fails to board the plane with the girls, Laura and Nicki find a note in the baby's diaper bag. Did the mother really abandon the child? Was the woman in the airport really the baby's mother, or was she a kidnapper? Nicki and her friends have only eight hours to find answers to their many questions about the baby in their care.

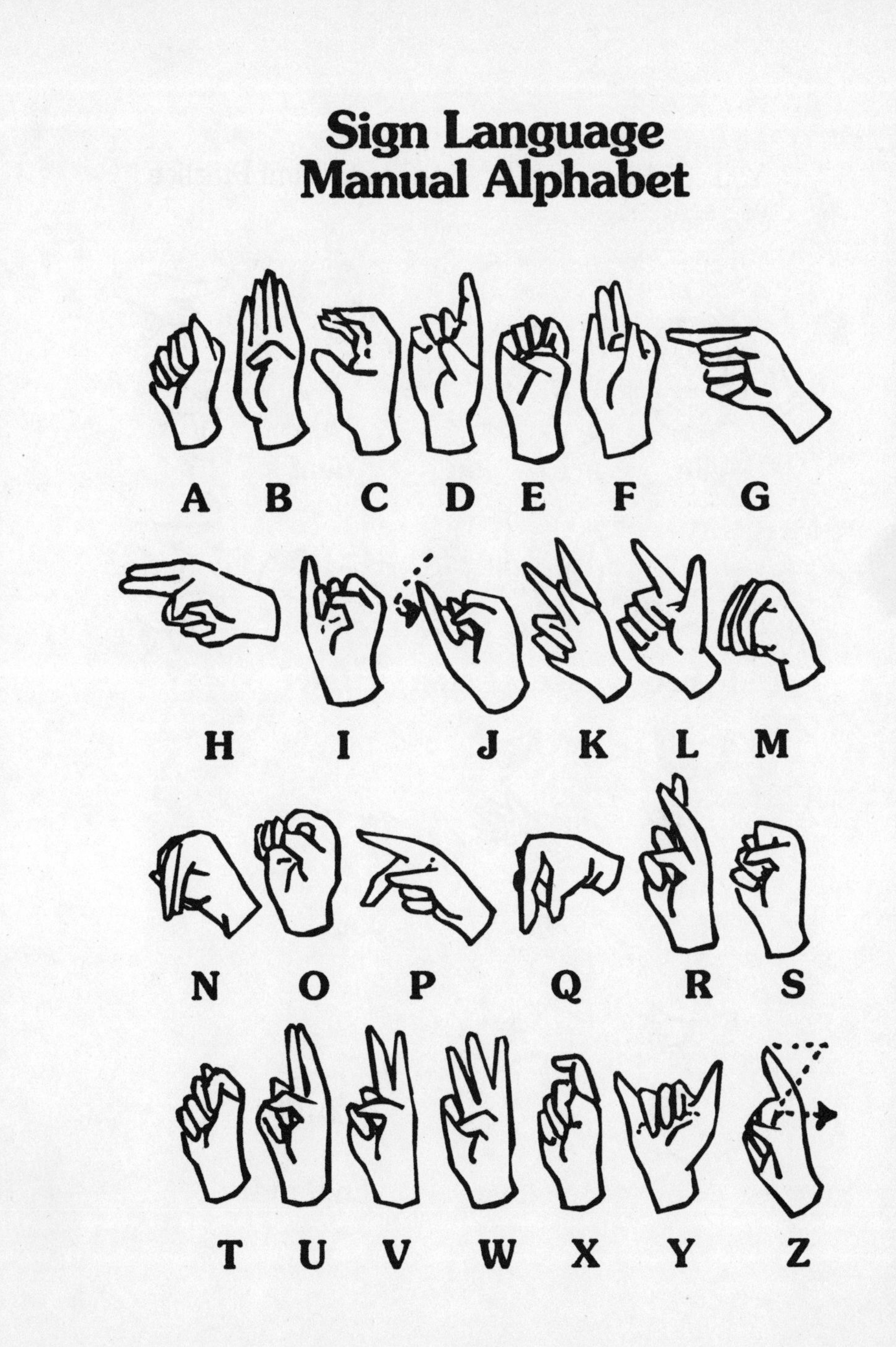
Sign Language
Manual Alphabet
A B C D E F G
H I J K L M
N O P Q R S
T U V W X Y Z

You can learn sign language with Kim! Practice these sentences:

I love England!